'I have always nurtured a sneaking suspicion that there was something slightly funny about Edam cheese, and Willem Elsschot's little book is absolute proof. It is brilliant. It has a wonderful Keatonesque comic pacing which is total bliss. I adored it' Glen Baxter

'Satirical and charming, this story of one man's fight to sell 10,000 tons of Edam deserves wider recognition' *Hampstead & Highgate Express*

'Full of sly irony and gentle satire, this is one "cheese" that has matured well since it first appeared in the 1930s' *Publishing News*

**Willem Elsschot** (1882–1960) was the pseudonym of Alfons De Ridder, head of a successful advertising agency who, unbeknownst to his family, was a best-selling novelist in his spare time. *Cheese*, his breakthrough work, was first published in Dutch in 1933.

**Paul Vincent** taught Dutch language and literature for many years at London University before becoming a full-time translator in 1980. He has translated various modern Dutch prose writers, including Harry Mulisch, Margriet de Moor, J. Bernlef and H. M. van den Brink.

# CHEESE

*Willem Elsschot*

TRANSLATED AND WITH A PREFACE BY
*Paul Vincent*

**Granta Books**
London

Granta Publications, 2/3 Hanover Yard, Noel Road, London N1 8BE

Originally published in the Netherlands as *Kaas* 1933
First published in Great Britain by Granta Books 2002
This edition published by Granta Books 2003

A CIP catalogue record for this book
is available from the British Library.

3 5 7 9 10 8 6 4 2

Typeset by M Rules

Printed and bound in Great Britain
by Mackays of Chatham plc

# TRANSLATOR'S PREFACE

The works of Willem Elsschot are literary classics in the Low Countries. The Antwerp author, whose real name was Alfons de Ridder, published eleven short novels and a volume of poetry between 1913 and 1946.[1] Despite his occasionally problematic relationship with the literary world, Elsschot's popularity in the Netherlands and Belgium has grown steadily. Since the publication of the *Collected Works* in 1957, he has been constantly in print. His works have also been translated into over twenty languages, and there have been many theatrical and film adaptations –

---

1 Two previous translations have appeared in English: *Three Novels: Soft Soap / The Leg / Will-o'-the-Wisp* (tr. A. Brotherton), Leiden/London/New York: Sijthoff/Heinemann/London House & Maxwell, 1965; *Villa des Roses* (tr. with an introduction and notes by P. Vincent), Harmondsworth: Penguin Books, 1992.

most recently Orlow Seunke's TV version of *Cheese* (2000).

The author, with a large family to support, spent most of his working life in advertising; writing was a secondary, though hugely important, pursuit. In fact, by 1933, the year when *Cheese* was written and published, Elsschot had not produced a book for ten years, disappointed as he was by the poor sales and critical neglect of its predecessor *Soft Soap*, 1923. Here an earlier incarnation of the Laarmans character becomes the acolyte of the Mephistophelian advertising salesman Boorman, himself a supporting player in Chapter XVI of *Cheese*. Encouraged by the editors of the Belgo-Dutch literary magazine *Forum,* especially the Dutch writer Jan Greshoff (to whom the book is dedicated), Elsschot completed at whirlwind speed, within some two weeks, the novel he persisted in regarding as his best work.[2]

Elsschot's private comments on the book are illuminating. Writing to Greshoff, he describes 'the cheese business' as 'just a pretext to be able to dredge things up from my own depths'.[3] He made his fullest, almost Flaubertian, pronouncement to another editor

2 See letters such as that in Willem Elsschot, *Brieven,* V. van de Reijt & L. Paris (eds), Amsterdam, 1993, p. 605.

3 *Brieven,* p. 102.

of *Forum*, the critic Menno ter Braak: 'My intention was to make an extremely humdrum, completely run-of-the-mill event gripping through intensity. In other words, to make something out of nothing.'[4] This may seem a paradoxical position for a writer championed in *Forum* as an accessible, 'non-literary' voice, and with enduring reader appeal, but Elsschot made no secret of the fact that for him art, though concealed, underpinned the whole fictional structure, while emotion, though understated, was omnipresent.

A request from a producer for permission to make a stage adaptation prompts the gloomy response: 'I'm afraid he'll play it for laughs.'[5] This may seem an odd reaction, given the often richly comic efforts of the Quixotic/Walter Mitty–like Laarmans character to succeed in a business world for which he patently has little aptitude. However, Elsschot seems to suggest that a knockabout treatment would fail to do justice either to the deadly seriousness of the endeavour for Laarmans himself, or his sense of social inadequacy: these are undoubtedly a source of humour, but at the same time of toe-curling pathos. More gratifying to the author was a favourable review of the Dutch edition

---

4 *Brieven*, p.179.
5 *Brieven*, p. 159.

of *Cheese* in the *Times Literary Supplement* of 26 April 1934, which praised the book as a moving 'tragi-comedy, set against a lightly sketched background of Flemish middle-class life'.[6]

Long after the appearance of *Cheese,* Elsschot ghosted a school essay on his own work for his grandson, in which he claimed that malodorous cheese was a metaphor in the novel for the distasteful advertising business, in which both the author and (in other books) his character Laarmans are involved. This interpretation became the received wisdom. However, it has been persuasively argued by Guido Lauwaert that this is a false trail, or at most a very partial view.[7] After all, De Ridder was a shrewd and successful businessman. For Lauwaert the book reflects Elsschot's uncomfortable encounters with the literary and publishing establishment, and the stacks of cheeses languishing in the warehouse suggest the piles of unsold copies of *Soft Soap* that cluttered De Ridder's own attic. He points particularly to the new chapter (XV), added for the novel's third edition in 1941, in which he plausibly identifies no less than four members of the editorial board of *Forum* in the cheese

6 *Brieven*, p. 185.

7 Guido Lauwaert, *Villa Elsschot*, Amsterdam: Guido Lauwaert & Uitgeverij Bas Lubberhuizen, 1991, p. 31.

traders' delegation to the ministry. In this scene Laarmans, the outsider, wins the negotiations through his direct tactics, but still feels alienated from and used by the veteran professionals. The somewhat acrimonious demise of *Forum* in 1935 and Elsschot's loss of contact with most of the former editors may well have inspired this disguised satire on the literary world. Further reason, if any were needed, for not identifying the writer and his creation.

Elsschot never saw himself as a man of letters: though he gave successful readings from his own work — at which he was famously often close to tears, despite the mirth of the audience — and had close friendships with a number of writers, he never relished the literary circuit. The author's working library consisted largely of the Bible and Shakespeare and he was frequently forced to appeal to his children for copies of his books. Nor, despite comments in his letters, interviews and the 'Afterword' to *Cheese* (called an 'Introduction' and preceding the novel in the Dutch editions, though written after its completion), can he be called a literary theorist or intellectual. In one of the most disarming passages in the letters he asks Greshoff: 'Who is this *Freud* they're always talking about in Forum? Can you recommend one of his books?'[8]

---

8 *Brieven*, p. 183.

On its appearance in 1913, Elsschot's hilarious and heart-rending début *Villa des Roses*, set in the eponymous seedy Paris boarding-house, was in clear contrast to the dominant tradition of self-conscious, even militant, rural Flemishness prevalent at the time. With one exception, the novel *Deliverance* (1920), Elsschot's backdrop is consistently urban. His style too is spare rather than lushly evocative like that of the internationally known novelist Louis Couperus. While recognisably Flemish, his language aspires to a more neutral, widely comprehensible Dutch, possibly influenced by a period spent working in Rotterdam before the First World War.

Elsschot's ironic humour, restraint and economy would seem calculated to appeal to an English-speaking readership. The anonymous *Times Literary Supplement* reviewer of *Cheese* was struck by the book's lightness of touch. Minimalism ('. . . when one character will do a crowd of them is superfluous', as Elsschot says in his 'Introduction') and understatement are major tools but overlay powerful emotional undercurrents. Elsschot never strayed from his belief in the power of style over content, as expressed in the 'Introduction':

> In nature tragedy resides in the event itself. In art it resides more in the style than in what happens. A herring can be depicted in a tragic light, although there is nothing inherently tragic about such a creature.

> On the other hand it is not sufficient to say 'my old
> father is dead' to achieve a tragic effect.

Simple yet profound words which might seem glib
without the *oeuvre* they accompany, but which have
resonated with generations of readers – and fellow-
writers – in the Low Countries and beyond.

The narrative framework of *Cheese* is ostensibly a
series of letters from the protagonist, a lowly clerk in
a shipyard, to an unnamed correspondent, documenting
Laarmans' brief, ill-starred attempt to establish himself
in business as the representative in 'Belgium and the
Grand Duchy of Luxembourg' of a Dutch cheese
exporter – in fact he dislikes the product – before
retreating traumatised to his old job and the bosom of
his family. The recurring figure of Laarmans had made
his first appearance in the novel *Soft Soap* and its
sequel *The Leg* as an idealistic Flemish militant turned
apprentice business shark. As a restless paterfamilias
he was to feature in Elsschot's final masterpiece *Will-o'-
the-Wisp*, combing the Antwerp docks with a group
of Afghan sailors for the address of a whore.

Through the eyes of the status-obsessed Laarmans
the reader is given brief but telling glimpses of the
rigid class system of the time (the gatherings at the
house of Van Schoonbeke), and of the desperate social
conditions of the Depression (the response to his call

for agents). Laarmans has elements of the 'little man' depicted by Chaplin and Keaton, but is at once less lovable, with his underlying rage and rancour, and more vulnerable, revealing his inner insecurities at every turn. For a writer unfamiliar with Freud, Elsschot has painted a remarkable portrait of a mother-obsessed figure failing to live up to his own aspirations, a worthy companion to Italo Svevo's Zeno in twentieth-century literature's gallery of failures.

## To Jan Greshoff

Silent, I listen to the hoarse
and panting voice, its force,
singing in a minor key,
cursing mediocrity.

The corners of his mouth I watch,
like a wound the surgeon's botched,
which when it laughs says everything
that he expressed with such a sting.

He has a wife, kids, friendships too
and many more to whom he's true,
whom he treasures as his own.
Yet Jan Greshoff stands alone.

He looks, hopes, waits and seeks a way,
the whole night long and through the day.
He hears a noise and sits up straight:
he waits in Brussels for his fate.

Go on, Jan lad, don't spare the lash
and punish all the rotten trash!
Sweep all those cattle from your road
while you've the heart to bear the load.

# CAST OF CHARACTERS

Frans Laarmans, *a clerk with the General Marine and Shipbuilding Company, thereafter a businessman, and finally a clerk again*

Laarmans' mother (*senile and dying*)

Dr Laarmans, *Frans' brother*

Mr Van Schoonbeke, *a friend of the doctor and the cause of all the trouble*

Hornstra, *an Amsterdam cheese merchant*

Fine, *Laarmans' wife*

Jan and Ida, *their children*

Mrs Peeters, *a bilious neighbour*

Hamer, *head bookkeeper at General Marine*

Anna van der Tak  
Tuil  
Erfurt  } *clerks with General Marine*  
Bartherotte

Boorman, *a business consultant*

Old Piet, *an engine driver with General Marine*

Young Van der Zijpen, *who wants to go into partnership*
Friends of Van Schoonbeke

# ELEMENTS

*Cheese. Cheese dream. Cheese movie. Cheese business. Cheese day. Cheese campaign. Cheese world. Cheese ship. Cheese trade. Cheese line. Cheese adventure. Cheese-eaters. Cheeseman. Cheese round. Cheese trader. Cheese trust. Cheese dragon. Cheese misery. Cheese will. Cheese fantasy. Cheese wall. Cheese question. Cheese lorry. Cheese ordeal. Cheese tower. Cheese wound.*

GAFPA (General Antwerp Feeding Products Association)

Cellar of haulage firm

Laarmans' office, complete with telephone, desk and typewriter

A backgammon set

A wicker suitcase

A large cheese shop

A cemetery

---

# 1

I'm writing to you again at last because great things are about to happen, and it's all Mr van Schoonbeke's doing.

I should tell you that my mother has died.

A nasty business of course, not only for her, but also for my sisters, as the vigil nearly killed them.

She was old, very old. I don't remember precisely how old to the exact year. She wasn't really ill, just thoroughly worn out.

My eldest sister, with whom she lived, was good to her. She soaked her bread in milk, made sure she went to the toilet, and gave her potatoes to peel to keep her occupied. She peeled and peeled as though she had an army to feed. We all took our potatoes to my sister's, and on top of that Mother did the lady's upstairs and a couple more neighbours' besides, because once, when they'd tried giving her a bucket of potatoes that were already peeled to repeel, because stocks were low, she'd noticed and actually said, 'They've already been peeled.'

When she couldn't peel any more, because she could no longer co-ordinate her hands and eyes very well, my sister gave her wool and kapok which had been compressed into little hard lumps through having been slept on, to pick apart. It made a lot of dust and Mother herself was covered in fluff from head to toe.

It went on and on, day and night: dozing, picking, dozing, picking. Punctuated by the occasional smile, God knows at whom.

She couldn't remember a thing about my father, who'd only been dead about five years, even though they'd had nine children together.

When I went to visit her, I used to talk about him occasionally to try and put a spark of life in her.

I'd ask her if she really couldn't remember Chris (that had been his name).

She made a terrific effort to follow what I was on about. She seemed to grasp that she needed to grasp something, leaned forward in her chair, and stared at me with her face all tense and the veins in her temples bulging: like a guttering lamp threatening to go out with a bang.

After a little while the spark would be extinguished again and she'd give you that smile that went right through you. If I pressed her too hard she'd get frightened.

No, the past no longer existed for her. There was no Chris, no children, just picking kapok.

There was only one thing that still played on her mind: the thought that a last little mortgage on one of her houses hadn't been paid off yet. Was she trying to scrape together that piffling amount before she went?

My sister, bless her, would talk about her, while she was present, like someone who wasn't there: 'She ate well. She's been very tiresome today.'

When she couldn't pick any more she sat for a time with her blue, gnarled hands placed parallel on her lap or scratching at her chair for hours as though she couldn't stop picking. She could no longer tell yesterday from tomorrow. All that either of them meant was 'not now'. Was it because her sight was failing or because she was tormented by evil spirits the whole time? At any rate, she no longer knew whether it was day or night, and got up when she should have been in bed and went to sleep when she was supposed to talk.

If she held on to walls and furniture, she could still walk a bit. At night when everyone was asleep, she'd totter over to her chair and start picking kapok that wasn't there, or hunt till she found the coffee grinder, as though she were about to make coffee for some crony or other.

And she'd always have that black hat on her grey head, even at night. Do you believe in witchcraft?

Finally she lay down and when she calmly allowed the hat to be taken off, I knew she wouldn't be getting up again.

## 2

That evening I'd played cards in the Three Kings till midnight and drunk four or so pale ales, so I was in perfect shape to sleep right through the night.

I tried to get undressed as quietly as possible, as my wife had been in bed for ages and I don't like all that nagging.

But when I stood on one leg to get my first sock off, I fell against the bedside table and she woke with a start.

'You should be ashamed of yourself,' she began.

And then the front doorbell sounded right through our silent house, making my wife sit up.

There's something solemn about a ring like that at night.

We both waited till the jangling in the stairwell had died away, I with heart pounding and my right foot in my hands.

'Whatever can that be?' she whispered. 'Go and

have a look out of the window, you're only half
undressed.'

That wasn't the way things usually ended up, but
the bell had stopped her in her tracks.

'If you don't go and look this instant, I'll go myself,'
she threatened.

But I knew what it was. What else could it be?

Outside I saw a shadowy figure standing at our
door who called up that he was Oscar and asked me
to come straight to Mother with him. Oscar is one of
my brothers-in-law, a man who's indispensable on
occasions like this.

I told my wife the reason for the ring, put my
clothes back on and went and opened the door.

'It'll be tonight,' guaranteed my brother-in-law.
'She's in her death throes. And put a scarf on, it's
cold.'

I did as he said and went with him.

Outside it was quiet and clear, and we walked
briskly along like two people on their way to some
nightshift job or other.

When we reached the house I automatically
reached for the bell, but Oscar stopped me, asked me
if I was off my head, and rattled the letterbox gently.

My niece, a daughter of Oscar, let us in. She closed
the door behind us without a sound and said I should
go up, which I did behind Oscar. I'd taken my hat off,
which I didn't usually do when I went to see Mother.

My brother, my three sisters and the lady from upstairs were sitting together in the kitchen, next to the room where she must still be lying. Where else could she be lying?

An old nun, another cousin of ours, glided inaudibly out of the room where the dying woman was, into the kitchen and then back again.

They all looked at me as though I'd something to answer for, and one of them whispered a welcome.

Was I supposed to sit or stand?

If I stood it was as though I was ready to leave again immediately, and if I sat down, it was as though I were taking it all in my stride, including what was happening to Mother. But as they were all seated, I got a chair too and stayed at the back, out of the light of the lamp. The atmosphere was unusually tense. Perhaps because they had stopped the clock?

It was damned hot in the kitchen. And on top of that there was the bunch of women with swollen eyes, as though they'd been peeling onions.

I didn't know what to say.

It was no good asking how Mother was, as everyone knew she was fading fast.

Crying would have been the best thing to do, but how was I supposed to start? Just give a sudden sob? Or get out my handkerchief and dab my eyes, whether they were wet or not?

That wretched pale ale was now finally beginning to take effect, obviously because of the heat in the kitchen, and made me break out in a sweat.

So as to have something to do I stood up. 'Go and have a look,' said my brother, who's a doctor.

He spoke normally, not too loud, but just loud enough for me to be sure that my nocturnal journey had not been for nothing. I followed his advice, as I was frightened of being sick from all that beer, and the heat and the mood in the kitchen. They would probably put it down to emotion, but just imagine if I'd started throwing up.

It was cooler and almost dark in there, to my relief.

On the bedside table there was a solitary candle which did not light up mother in her high bed, so I wasn't upset by her death agony. Our cousin the nun was sitting praying.

When I'd stood there for a while my brother came in too, picked up the candle, held it up like in a torch-light procession and lit up Mother.

He must have seen something, because he went into the kitchen and asked everyone to come in.

I heard chairs being pushed back and there they all were.

A moment later my sister said that it was over, but the nun contradicted her, saying that the two tears hadn't yet fallen. Were they supposed to come from Mother?

It went on for a good hour, with me still full of beer, but finally she was pronounced dead.

And they were right, for however hard I silently willed her to sit up and make the whole lot of them scatter with that fearsome smile of hers, it was no good. She lay as still as only the dead can lie.

It had gone pretty fast and I nearly hadn't made it in time.

I went completely cold when the women's chorus started wailing, and couldn't join in.

Where on earth did they get all those tears from, for they weren't the first, I could tell from their faces. Fortunately my brother wasn't crying either. But he's a doctor and we all know that he's used to such scenes, so it was still embarrassing for me.

I tried to make up for everything by hugging the womenfolk and shaking their hands firmly. I thought it was outrageous that she should have been alive just a short while ago and wasn't any longer.

And suddenly my sisters stopped crying, fetched water, soap and towels, and started washing her.

The effect of the beer had now completely worn off, which proves that I was moved at least as deeply as the others.

I went back and sat in the kitchen till they'd finished her toilet, and then we were called back to her bedside.

They had worked hard in that short time and the precious corpse now looked better than it had while still alive and laughing to itself as it peeled or picked. 'Auntie looks really beautiful,' said our cousin the nun, gazing with satisfaction at the bed with Mother in it.

And she should know, since she's in an order at Lier, the kind that means that from her youth to her last breath she is sent from one sick person to another, and so spends all her time sitting next to corpses.

Then my niece made coffee, which the women had earned, and Oscar was given permission to entrust the funeral arrangements to a friend of his who according to him was as good and as cheap as anyone else. 'That's fine, Oscar,' my eldest sister said with a weary gesture, as though she were not the least interested in the question of price.

I saw that the gathering was about to break up but didn't really dare to take the lead, as I'd been the last to arrive.

One of my sisters yawned while still shedding a few tears, whereupon my brother put his hat on, shook hands with everyone again and left.

'I may as well go with Karel,' I said at this point. They were the first words I uttered, I think. Perhaps they would give the impression that I was going for Karel's sake, for even a doctor might be in need of comfort, mightn't he?

And so I was able to get out of the house.

It was three o'clock by the time I was back in our

bedroom holding one foot in my hand and taking off my first sock. I was asleep on my feet, and so as not to have to tell the whole story I just said there was no change.

There's not much to say about the funeral. It went off quite normally and I wouldn't be mentioning it, the whole business of my mother's death, if it weren't for the fact that that was how I came into contact with Mr Van Schoonbeke.

As is customary my brother, myself, my brothers-in-law and four cousins were standing in a semicircle around the coffin, before it was taken away. More distant relatives, and friends and acquaintances then came in and shook hands with each of us with a whispered word of condolence or a fixed stare, straight in the eye. There were lots of them, far too many really, I thought, since it went on and on.

My wife had put a black armband on my arm, as I had agreed with my brother not to have a mourning suit specially made, seeing as you have so little use for it after the funeral. And the wretched armband must have been too big as it kept slipping down. Every three or four handshakes I had to push it back up. And then Mr Van Schoonbeke came, who was a friend and also a patient of my brother. He did the same as the others but was much more chic and modest about it. I could tell he was a man of the world.

He went to the church and the cemetery with us and got into one of the carriages with my brother and me. I was introduced to him and he invited me to call on him. Which I did.

# 3

That Mr Van Schoonbeke comes from an old and wealthy family. He's a bachelor and lives alone in a big house in one of our nicest streets.

He's got bags of money, and all of his friends have money too. They're mostly judges, lawyers, business-men or ex-businessmen. Every member of the group has at least one car, except for Mr Van Schoonbeke, my brother and me. But Mr Van Schoonbeke could afford a car if he wanted, and no one knows that better than his friends. Which is why they find it strange and sometimes say 'funny old Albert'.

With my brother and myself it was a different matter.

As a doctor he has no valid excuse for not having a car, all the more so as he cycles, thus making clear that he travels enough to need one. But for us barbarians a doctor is sacred, on a par with priests, so by virtue of his being a doctor my brother is more or less presentable, even without a car. For in the circles he moves in Mr Van Schoonbeke really has no business cultivating friends without money or status.

When they come in and catch him with a stranger, he introduces the newcomer in such a way that they all think at least a hundred per cent more of the man than he's really worth. He calls a head of department a manager and introduces a colonel in civvies as a general.

But I was a difficult case.

As you know I'm a clerk with the General Marine and Shipbuilding Company, so he had nothing to latch on to. There's nothing sacred about a clerk. He's naked in the world.

He thought for a couple of seconds, no longer, and then introduced me as 'Mr Laarmans from the shipbuilding yards'.

He considers the English name of our company too long to remember and also too precise, for he knows that in every single large firm in town at least one of his friends knows someone on the board who could inform him immediately of my social insignificance. He would never have dreamt of saying 'clerk', as that would have been my death knell. And for the rest I had to get by as best I could. He had given me that coat of chain mail, but he could do no more.

16

'So you're an engineer?' asked a man with gold teeth sitting next to me.

'An inspector,' said my friend Van Schoonbeke, knowing that being an engineer involves a particular university, a degree and far too much technical knowledge for it not to cause me problems in my first conversation.

I laughed, to make them think that there was a big secret about it which might be revealed when the moment was ripe.

They sneaked a glance at my suit, which was thankfully almost new and could pass muster, even though it wasn't particularly well cut, and proceeded to ignore me.

They first talked about Italy, where I've never been, and I travelled with them through the whole land of Goethe's Mignon: Venice, Milan, Florence, Rome, Naples, Vesuvius and Pompeii. I've read about it, but Italy remains just a dot on the map to me, so I kept silent. Nothing was said about the artistic treasures, but Italian women were marvellous and passionate, apparently.

When they had had enough of that, they discussed the difficult situation of landlords. A lot of houses were standing empty and they all maintained that their tenants paid irregularly. I wanted to protest, not on behalf of my tenants, as I haven't got any, but because I myself have always paid on time up to now, but by that time they had already got on to their cars: four and six cylinders, garage charges, petrol and oil, things that I of course know nothing about.

Next a survey was given of what had happened during the past week in those families worth mentioning.

'The Gevers boy got married to Legrelle's daughter,' said one.

It isn't mentioned as a news item, because everyone already knows apart from me, but rather as an item on the agenda on which a vote is necessary. They either approve or disapprove, depending on whether or not both parties are bringing equal fortunes to the match.

They're all of the same opinion, so no time is wasted on discussion. Each of them expresses only collective thought.

'So Delafaille has resigned as chairman of the Chamber of Commerce.'

I've never heard of the man, but they not only know he exists and has resigned, but usually also know the real reason behind it: official odium because of bankruptcy, some secret illness or other, a scandal involving his wife or daughter, or simply because he was fed up with the job.

Going through the 'agenda items' takes up the greater part of the evening and is the most uncomfortable time for me, as I have to limit myself to nodding, laughing or raising my eyebrows.

I'm in a constant panic, and sweating more than when Mother died. You now know how I suffered then, but at least that was over in one night, while at Van Schoonbeke's it starts all over again every week, and the sweat I've already shed isn't subtracted from what still lies in store for me.

As they have nothing to do with me outside my friend's place, they can't remember my name, and at the beginning they gave me all kinds of names which only vaguely resembled my real one. And since I couldn't keep correcting them by repeatedly saying 'Sorry, it's Laarmans,' they finally started looking at my friend Van Schoonbeke first and saying to him, in my presence, 'Your friend maintains that the Liberals . . .' or somesuch. And only then would they look in my direction. That made the use of my name unnecessary. And at the same time 'your friend' implies that van Schoonbeke has some fine friends nowadays.

In fact they prefer me to say nothing at all, because whenever I say anything it means a whole palaver for one of them. Out of politeness to the host, one of them is obliged to give me a sketch of the birth, childhood, studies, marriage and career of some local celebrity or other, whose funeral was all they wanted to discuss that evening.

I can't stand restaurants either.

'Last week I had snipe with my wife in the Trois Perdrix in Dijon.'

Why he should say that his wife was there too, I
have no idea.

'So, a dirty weekend with your lawful wedded wife,
lad,' says someone else.

And then they start mentioning restaurants, com-
peting with each other, not only in Belgium but far
and wide abroad too.

The first time, when I wasn't yet so shy, I felt it my
duty to mention one too, in Dunkirk. A schoolfriend
had told me years ago that he had once dined there on
his honeymoon. And I had remembered it because it
was named after a famous pirate.

I kept my restaurant at the ready and waited for an
appropriate moment.

But by this time they were talking about Saulieu,
Dijon, Grenoble, Digne, Grasse and were obviously
on their way to Nice and Monte Carlo, so I could
scarcely mention Dunkirk. It would have been like
suddenly bringing up Tilburg while the restaurants on
the Riviera were being summed up.

'Believe it or not, but last week in Rouen, at the
Vieille Horloge, I had a selection of hors d'oeuvres,
lobster, half a chicken with truffles, cheese and dessert,
all for thirty francs,' said someone suddenly.

'The lobster wasn't tinned Japanese crab by any
chance, old man, was it?' someone asked.

'And the truffles minced prostate?'

Rouen isn't that far from Dunkirk and it was a

perfect chance that I couldn't let pass. So I took advantage of the next silence and suddenly said, 'The Jean-Bart in Dunkirk is excellent too.'

Even though I'd geared myself up for it, I was alarmed by the sound of my own voice.

I lowered my eyes and waited for the reaction.

Fortunately I hadn't claimed that I'd eaten there myself in the last few weeks, because someone immediately said that the Jean-Bart had been closed for about three years and was now a cinema.

Yes, the more I say, the more clearly they can see not only that I do not have a car, but I never will have one. So silence is the best policy, since they're beginning to keep an eye on me and must be wondering how Van Schoonbeke came to be offering me his hospitality. If it were not for my brother, who occasionally gets patients through Van Schoonbeke, I'd have sent the whole lot of them packing long ago.

Week by week it became clearer to me that my friend was finding me a troublesome protégé, and that it couldn't go on like this, when suddenly last Wednesday he asked me if I was at all interested in becoming the Belgian representative for a big Dutch firm. They were very enterprising people, for whom he had just won a big court case. I could get the job right away. It would suffice for him to put in a word, and he was very happy to do so. No money was needed.

'Think about it,' he advised me. 'There's a lot of money to be made and you're the right man.'

That was a bit presumptuous of him, because I don't think anyone should think I'm the right man before I think so myself. But still it was nice of him to give me the chance with no strings attached of shedding my togs as a simple clerk with the General Marine and Shipbuilding Company and becoming a businessman overnight. His friends would be bound to drop fifty per cent of their haughtiness. Just because they had a penny or two!

So I asked him what kind of business his Dutch friends were in.

'Cheese,' said my friend. 'And there's always a market for that, since people have to eat.'

## 4

On my way home in the tram I already felt like a new man.

As you know I'm getting on for fifty, and my thirty years of servility have naturally left their mark on me.

Clerks are humble, much humbler than workmen, who have extracted a modicum of respect through their rebelliousness. They even say that in Russia they've taken over. If it's true then they've deserved it, I reckon. Come to that, they seem to have paid for it with their blood. But clerks aren't generally very specialised and are so interchangeable that even a man with years of experience may get a kick up his fifty-year-old backside and be replaced by someone else who's every bit as good and much cheaper.

Since I know that and have children, I'm careful to avoid getting into arguments with strangers, as they may be friends of my boss. So I let myself be jostled on the tram and don't get too worked up if someone treads on my toes.

But that evening I couldn't care less about any of that. After all, wasn't the cheese dream about to come true?

I could sense that I already had a more resolute look in my eyes, and I put my hands in my trouser pockets with a nonchalance that had been totally unknown to me half an hour before.

When I got home I sat down quite normally at the table and had supper without saying a word about the new opportunity that had presented itself, and had to laugh to myself when I saw my wife spreading butter and cutting the bread with her usual thriftiness. Well, she wasn't to know that tomorrow she might be the wife of a businessman.

I ate as I usually did, no more or less, no more hurriedly or slowly. In a word, I ate like someone resigned to the fact that his years of bondage at the General Marine and Shipbuilding Company will have to be extended by an indefinite number of further years.

But still my wife asked what was the matter with me.

'Why should anything be the matter with me?' I asked back.

And then I began to look at my two children's homework.

---

I spotted a glaring error in a French past participle and corrected it so breezily and amiably that my son looked up in surprise.

'What are you looking at, Jan?' I asked.

'I don't know,' said the boy, laughing and casting a glance of complicity at my wife.

So he too seemed to notice something different about me. And to think that I had always believed I was a master at hiding my feelings. Well, I'll just have to learn how to, as it will certainly come in handy in business. And if my face is such an open book, then during the 'agenda' bulletins there must have been murderous things to read on it.

I think the marital bed is the best place for discussing serious matters. At least you're alone with your wife then. The blankets muffle the sound of voices, darkness helps reflection, and since you can't see each other, neither of you is influenced by the other's emotion. One is able to say all those things one doesn't really dare to say to someone's face, and so it was there that, having settled nicely on my right side, after an introductory silence, I told my wife I was going into business.

Since all she's had to listen to for years have been fatuous confidences, she made me repeat what I'd said and waited for a fuller explanation, which I gave her in calm, clear, and, I might as well say it, businesslike terms. In the space of five minutes she was given a general picture of Van Schoonbeke's circle of friends and their natural, unconscious habit of belittling others, and of the parting proposal with which he had so unexpectedly sent me on my way home.

My wife listened carefully, keeping as quiet as a mouse, without once coughing or turning over. And when I'd finished she asked me what I intended to do and whether I planned to give up my job with the General Marine and Shipbuilding Company.

'Yes,' I said casually, 'I'll have to. One can't possibly be a clerk somewhere and at the same time be in business for oneself. One's got to make a firm decision.'

'What about in the evenings?' came the question, after a new silence.

'It's dark in the evenings,' I said.

That one hit home, as the bed creaked and my wife turned over as though she had decided to let me stew in my business plans. So I had to chip in again myself.

'What do you mean, in the evenings?' I snapped.

'You could do business in the evenings,' she persisted. 'What kind of business is it?'

I had to admit that it was in cheese. It's strange, but to me there was something revolting and ridiculous about this commodity. I'd have preferred it if I could have traded in something else, flowers, for example, or light bulbs, which after all are also specifically Dutch. I'd even have been keener on selling herring – preferably the dried sort – than cheese. But I realised that the firm from up north couldn't very well change its business just to please me.

'Funny thing to sell, isn't it?' I asked.

But my wife disagreed on that point.

'There's always a market for it,' she said, just like Van Schoonbeke had.

Her encouragement gave me a shot in the arm and I said that I was going to tell the General Marine and Shipbuilding Company the very next morning that it could go to hell. I was just going to go into the office to say goodbye to my colleagues.

'For goodness' sake start by applying for the agency,' said my wife. 'And then you can work out what you've got to do. You're like a man possessed.'

That last remark showed precious little respect for a businessman, but the advice was sound. For that matter, I may have said what I said about resigning, but that doesn't mean that I would have done it. When you've got a wife and children to support, you've got to be doubly careful.

The next day I went and got the name and address from my friend Van Schoonbeke, as well as a note of recommendation, and that same evening I wrote a lengthy, businesslike letter to Amsterdam, one of the best letters I've ever written. I posted it personally, as one can't entrust matters like that to anyone else, not even one's own children.

The answer was not long in coming. It arrived so quickly – in the shape of a telegram – that I was quite alarmed: 'Expect you tomorrow eleven o'clock head office Amsterdam. Will pay travel expenses.'

I now had to think up some reason for not going to work the next day, and my wife suggested a funeral. But I didn't like that idea, because I'd only recently taken a day off for Mother's funeral. You can hardly stay home for just any old cousin, at least not all day.

'Say you're ill then,' said my wife. 'You can prepare the ground today. There's enough flu about.'

So I sat with my head in my hands at the office and tomorrow I'm off to Amsterdam to make the acquaintance of Hornstra & Co.

# 5

The cheese movie has begun. Hornstra has appointed me sole representative for Belgium and the Grand Duchy of Luxembourg. '*Official* representative,' he calls it, though I'm not quite sure what he means. He just threw in the Grand Duchy as if he needed to make up the weight. True, it's a long way from Antwerp, but at least I get to see that hilly country. And the first chance I get I'll dish up some restaurants in Echternach, Diekirch and Vianden to those chaps at Van Schoonbeke's.

It was a pleasant journey. Since Hornstra was paying the fare anyway I went second class instead of third. Subsequently I found out that they had expected first class. I also realised too late that I could have gone third class and pocketed the difference. But it wouldn't have been proper, especially not on first acquaintance.

I was so excited that I couldn't keep still for five

minutes and when customs asked me if I had anything to declare, I said jovially, 'Of course not!' But the official replied that 'of course not' wasn't an answer and that I must say yes or no. I realised at once that you've got to be careful with the Dutch. And that impression was confirmed at Hornstra's, as he didn't waste words and within half an hour I had been dismissed and paid and was back in the street with my contract in my pocket. My friend Van Schoonbeke's letter had been decisive, because when I went on about my personal qualities, Hornstra didn't even listen, but after putting the letter away he asked me how many tons I thought I could shift.

That was a tricky question. How much Dutch cheese was consumed in Belgium every year and what percentage of that total market would I be able to get my hands on? I hadn't the faintest idea. Do you suppose that 'shifting', as he calls it, is an easy business?

My years of service with General Marine and Shipbuilding Company didn't suggest an answer and I felt that it wasn't advisable to mention a figure.

'You'd be wise to start small,' Hornstra said suddenly, obviously feeling that I'd thought it over long enough. 'I'll send you twenty tons of full-fat Edam in our new patent packaging. And as you pay that off, I'll top up your stock.'

Thereupon he presented me with a contract for signature, which boils down to the following: I am to be his representative for five per cent of the selling price, a fixed salary of three hundred guilders, and expenses paid.

After I had signed he pressed the buzzer, got up, shook my hand and before I was even out of his office there was another visitor sitting in my chair.

When I got outside I was delirious and had to force myself not to sing out like Faust 'À moi les désirs, à moi les maˆtresses'.*

Three hundred guilders a month was more than twice my salary with General and Marine Shipbuilding, and I had long since reached my ceiling with them, so I had been expecting my first wage reduction for a year or so now. In our yard you go from nought to a hundred and then back to nought again.

And paid travel expenses! Before I'd got to the end of the street I'd realised that from now on our holidays will be at Hornstra's expense. In Dinant or La Roche I can always quickly pop into a cheese shop in the evenings.

I can remember virtually nothing about Amsterdam, as everything I saw there I saw as if intoxicated. Later I heard from other people about the number of

---

* 'Let mine be the desires, mine the mistresses' (A misquotation from Gounod's *Faust*, Act I.)

cyclists and tobacconist shops and how long, narrow and crowded the Kalverstraat is. I scarcely took the time to have dinner there, and caught the first train back to Belgium, I was in such a hurry to inform Van Schoonbeke and my wife of my good fortune.

The return journey seemed endless. There were obviously some businessmen among my fellow passengers, as two of them were poring over papers. One of them was even making notes in the margin with a gold fountain pen. I must have a pen like that too: you can't keep asking your customers for pen and ink to take down their orders with.

It wasn't beyond the bounds of possibility that the man was also in the cheese business. I glanced at his hand luggage up in the luggage rack, but it was no help.

He was a smartly dressed gentleman, with immaculate linen, silk socks and a gold lorgnette. Cheese or not cheese?

I couldn't possibly sit there in silence all the way to Antwerp, I'd have burst. I simply had to speak, or sing. And as singing on the train was out of the question, I took advantage of a stop in Rotterdam to observe that the economic situation in Belgium seemed to be improving somewhat.

He looked straight at me, as though he were using my face to do a multiplication sum, and uttered a short sound in a language I did not know. What do you make of these businesspeople?

As luck would have it, it was Wednesday and I arrived at about five o'clock. And since the weekly chitchat at Van Schoonbeke's place started at about six on Wednesdays, I went to his place so he could inform his friends of how I had gone up in the world.

What a shame my mother couldn't have waited till she'd seen that.

At any rate it would be a relief to Van Schoonbeke that that clerk with General Marine and Shipbuilding was a thing of the past.

On the way I stopped outside a cheese shop to admire the window display. In the bright light of a host of bulbs lay cheeses of all shapes, sizes and origins, next to and on top of each other. They had converged on this spot from all our neighbouring countries.

Huge Gruyères as big as millstones served as a base, and on top of them were Cheshires, Goudas, Edams and numerous varieties of cheese that were entirely unknown to me, some of the largest with bellies slit open and innards exposed. The Roqueforts and Gorgonzolas lewdly flaunted their mould, and a squadron of Camemberts let their pus ooze out freely.

An odour of decay wafted from the shop, but this decreased after I had stood there for a while.

I didn't want to give way to the stink, and would only leave when I thought the time had come. A businessman must be as tough as a polar explorer.

'Go ahead and stink all you want,' I said defiantly.

If I'd had a whip I would have set about them.

'You're right, sir, it's unbearable,' replied a lady standing next to me, whose approach I hadn't heard.

I must get rid of the habit of thinking aloud on the public highway, since I've given people a scare on more than one occasion. That doesn't matter much with an anonymous clerk, but it's different with a businessman.

I hurried off to my friend Van Schoonbeke's, who congratulated me on my success and introduced me to his friends as if it was the first time they'd seen me.

'Mr Laarmans, a wholesale grocery merchant.' Then he filled the glasses.

Why had he said 'grocery' rather than 'cheese'? So he seemed to have something against that product, just like me.

As for me, I had to overcome it as soon as possible, for a businessman must be familiar with his product and identify with it. He has to live with it. He's got to be up to his ears in it. He's got to smell of it. That last bit wouldn't have been difficult in the case of cheese, but I meant it more in a figurative sense.

All things considered, cheese, apart from the smell, is a noble product, don't you agree? It's been made for centuries and it's one of the most important sources of wealth for the Dutch, who are a brother people. It feeds great and small, young and old. Something that is eaten by human beings acquires a certain nobility in the process. I believe Jews bless the food they eat, and why shouldn't a Christian say grace before eating cheese?

In any case my colleagues who dealt in fertilisers had a lot more to complain about. Fish waste, the entrails of mammals, carrion and suchlike. At least they too are dealt in till they render a final service to mankind.

Among Van Schoonbeke's regular guests there were several businessmen, at least two of them in grain, as they had already talked about it. Why should cheese be treated as inferior to grain? I'd soon rid them of that prejudice. After all it's the one who sells most who rules the roost. The future lies open before me and I am firmly resolved to put heart and soul into cheese.

'There's a good place here, Mr Laarmans,' said the visitor whose manner I had always disliked most. Not the one with the teeth, but a chic, bald chap who spoke well and could be witty, even during the 'agenda' that I hated so much.

And he immediately made room for me, so that for the first time I was actually sitting in their midst. Up to now I had always occupied a corner at the end of the long table, in such a way that they couldn't look at me without turning round almost completely, because out of politeness they sat angled towards the host.

For the first time, too, I hooked my thumbs into my waistcoat pockets and drummed on my stomach in a military tempo like someone who knows what's what. Van Schoonbeke noticed and smiled approvingly in my direction.

The fact that they immediately turned the conversation to the field of business showed that they were beginning to take me seriously.

I didn't say a lot, but did say, among other things, 'There's always a market for foodstuffs,' and they all agreed with me.

I was repeatedly looked at, as though one of them were seeking my approval, which I invariably gave at once with an indulgent nod of the head. You've got to be accommodating with people, especially if you're a businessman. But so as not to keep agreeing with their chatter, I occasionally said 'That remains to be seen' for a change. Whereupon the fellow in question, who normally couldn't stand being contradicted, replied very obligingly 'Of course,' happy to have got off so lightly.

When I felt that my success was sufficient for one day, I suddenly said: 'And what about the restaurants, gentlemen? What gastronomic treats have we had this week?'

That was my great moment. The whole company looked at me with gratitude, glad that with a truly regal gesture I had directed them to their favourite area.

Up to then I had always been the last to leave, as I had never had the nerve to be the first to get up and disrupt the harmony of the seated gathering. Moreover, when they had all gone I had the chance to pour my heart out to Van Schoonbeke in private, apologising both for having done or said so little in the course of the evening, and for everything I had neglected to do or say. But this time I looked at my watch, said aloud, 'Well I never . . . a quarter past seven. Goodbye, gentlemen, enjoy your evening,' tripped round the table like a man in a hurry, shook hands with them all and left them sitting there, which is all they were good for.

Van Schoonbeke saw me out, gave me a friendly pat on the back and said that I had done splendidly.

'You made a big impression,' he assured me. 'Good luck with your cheese.'

Now that we were alone in the hall he called a cheese a cheese. Upstairs it was foodstuffs.

Well, cheese is cheese. And if I were a knight, my coat of arms would be three cheeses on a field of sable.

# 6

My wife was not treated to the news at once, but had to be patient till I had had supper. Because from now on I shan't be eating any more, I'll be lunching, dining or having supper. Let me say that I have an excellent wife, who is, moreover, an exemplary mother. But I feel that matters like these are beyond her competence. I am also bound to admit that I sometimes can't resist the temptation to taunt her till the tears come. Those tears do me good. I use her to vent my fits of rage at my social inferiority. And I took advantage of my last hours of servitude with General Marine and Shipbuilding to give her the full treatment one last time.

So I ate in silence till she finally lost her temper, not with me but with the cutlery. And after a final pause I saw her eyes clouding with tears, whereupon she went into the kitchen. I really love having a dramatic mood like that in the house occasionally.

I followed her into the kitchen, like a cockerel chasing a hen, and as I looked for my slippers, suddenly said, 'You know the cheese thing is all wrapped up.'

The fact is, I think she *ought* to have known.

She didn't reply, but started doing the washing-up, banging crockery and iron pots, while I, filling a pipe, finally reported on how I had got on in Amsterdam.

I embellished things a little, saying that I had really put one over on Hornstra with the contract.

'Read it, here's the document,' I concluded.

And I handed it to her, knowing in advance that she would only half understand the formal Dutch and that all that commercialese would make her head spin.

She dried her hands, took the paper and sat down in the living room with it.

For me, someone who has typed thousands of letters for General Marine and Shipbuilding, the whole matter was child's play, of course. But I deliberately stayed pottering about in the kitchen, because she needed to learn the hard way that drawing up such a contract is a far cry from spring-cleaning.

'Did pretty well, didn't I?' I asked from the kitchen after a few minutes.

When I received no answer, I peered into the living room to see whether by any chance she had fallen asleep over my contract.

But she wasn't asleep. I saw her reading intently,

with her nose right up to the paper, following the text with her index finger so as not to miss any lines. She had stopped at one of the clauses.

Well, the document wasn't so remarkable that she had to pore over it like the Treaty of Versailles. Cheese, five per cent, three hundred guilders, that was enough.

I went over to the radio, turned the dial and got the national anthem. It was as if they were playing it in my honour.

'Turn that thing off for a moment, otherwise I won't be able to follow anything,' said my wife.

And a moment later she asked why I had put in the contract that they could 'kick me out' whenever they liked.

That's my wife for you. At least she calls a cheese a cheese.

'What do you mean, kick me out?' I asked with annoyance.

She put her finger on clause nine, the last one, and I read: 'In the event of Mr Laarmans' activities on behalf of Mr Hornstra terminating, either at the request of Mr Laarmans himself or on Mr Hornstra's initiative, the former will have no claim to any kind of compensation, nor to any further monthly payments, as the latter are intended not as a salary, but as an advance on possible commission, from which they will be deducted.'

Damnation, that wasn't all that straightforward. And I realised now why she had spent so long over it. In Amsterdam and afterwards in the train I had read that clause, but in my enthusiasm I hadn't worried too much about its exact meaning.

'What does "on Mr Hornstra's initiative" mean?' she asked, her finger still on the sore spot.

'Initiative' is one of those words my wife doesn't understand. 'Initiative', 'constructive' and 'objective' are all the same to her. And try explaining just what that kind of word means.

So I simply said, 'Well, initiative means initiative,' and meanwhile I read the clause in question through again, word for word, over her shoulder, and I had to admit she was right. Come to that, Hornstra was right too, since he couldn't commit himself till the year two thousand, if I didn't manage to get rid of the cheese. But I still felt ashamed.

'Initiative means starting something, Mum,' called Jan, without looking up from his schoolbooks. It's a bit much, isn't it, when a whippersnapper of fifteen has the nerve to pipe up unasked while such serious matters are being discussed?

'Surely you understand that I can't go on drawing such a high salary indefinitely, without the obligation of selling the goods I have received on consignment within a reasonable period of time,' I declared. 'After all, that would be immoral.'

I know for sure she won't understand 'consignment' or 'immoral', I thought. I'll blind her with science.

'Anyway,' I said, 'there's nothing to fear. If sales go well, then Hornstra will want nothing more than to continue the arrangement till kingdom come. And reciprocity in chucking out works to my advantage too, as you never know whether one of Hornstra's competitors won't be along with even better terms, as soon as I make a name for myself in the market.'

Let that young monkey try explaining the meaning of 'consignment', 'immoral' and 'reciprocity'.

My wife handed the paper back to me. 'Of course there's no reason why it shouldn't go well,' she said comfortingly. 'You'll just have to work hard. But I'd still be careful if I were you. You've got security at the yard, and a fixed salary.'

That's a cliché if ever I heard one.

# 7

The upshot of our most recent bed council was that the cheese venture should proceed without my giving in my notice at the yard. My wife says that my brother the doctor can fix it. He'll have to provide a certificate that will get me three months off to rest and recover from some illness or other that he'll dream up. She thought of that all by herself.

Personally I reckon it's a half-hearted solution and that in cases like this you've got to do one thing or the other.

God damn it, you either mount a cheese campaign or you don't. And if you start by building escape routes, you won't get anywhere. Give it all you've got, is what I say!

But what can I do? She brought the children into it and they sided with her. And I have no desire to fight constant battles on the home front, on top of all the worries of the hectic business world.

I've talked to my brother about it.

He's twelve years older than me and has taken the place of father and mother since they've been gone.

That difference of twelve years is an unbridgeable gap. When I was just a young ragamuffin he was already grown up, and since those days the relationship has stayed the same. He protects me, ticks me off, encourages me and gives me advice as if I were still playing marbles in the street. I must say he's an active and enthusiastic chap, full of courage and a sense of duty, and happy with his lot. I don't know if he's really out visiting the sick from morning till night. But in any case he whizzes round town on his bike all day and comes charging into my place every afternoon. He thunders into the kitchen where my wife is standing cooking, lifting the lids to have a smell and a peek, noisily greets my two children, who adore him, asks after our health, gives us samples of medicines for all kinds of ailments, empties his glass and charges off again, without pausing for breath.

I had a hard job getting him to listen to part one of the cheese saga, as he's very impatient, keeps interrupting and is only interested in what he can do to help.

When he heard that my position with General Marine and Shipbuilding might be in jeopardy, his open face assumed a severe expression.

'That's serious, my boy, a bloody serious business.'

And suddenly he left me standing there and went into the kitchen.

'Do you think he's cut out for trade?' I heard him ask.

'Well,' said my wife, 'he's the one who should know.'

'A serious business,' he repeated.

'That's what I told him.'

That's what she said. She said that! Doesn't it make you feel like throwing her out of the window?

Meanwhile I'm left standing there like a complete nonentity.

I just had time to put the radio on by way of protest, when he came back on to the porch.

'If I were you, I'd think long and hard about it first, old boy.'

I finally succeeded in telling him that what I want is to try to get three months off, as he hadn't let me get that far with my story, even though I'd had four attempts.

Thereupon he gave me the choice of a number of suitable ailments. Personally he preferred nerves, because then I can walk about outside without my boss being able to say a word against it. And nerves don't frighten anyone off. 'If I so much as mention lungs and later you go back to the yard, you'll be avoided like the plague.' He's convinced that mining the cheese seam is just a novelty for me and that later I'll really go back to the office.

Then he gave me a certificate.

'You know best, lad,' he said, again shaking his head.

I'm already a different man!

I no longer feel at home in the yard, and as I type out my letters, which are about engineering and ship-building, I'm haunted by the thought of the full-cream Edam cheeses that will be rolling off the production line in a few days' time, and will soon arrive. I'm frightened of typing cheeses into our orders instead of whetstones and sheet iron.

I wasn't able to see Mr Henri on the first day, though, as I didn't have the nerve, and I took the cer-tificate back home with me. But I'll have to – those threatening cheeses are after me; I'm like a dog that's forced to swim whether it likes it or not.

This morning I called in to see Hamer. Officially he's our head bookkeeper, but he's actually a real fac-totum who thoroughly deserves Mr Henri's trust. To tell the truth, he's a man you can talk to. He rests on his elbow, puts his hand to his right ear, listens with-out looking at you, and starts shaking his head.

I showed him my certificate and asked for advice, as I know that he likes nothing better than giving advice. Every day he has his surgery, like a doctor, and is con-sulted so much that he sees it as an admission of his superiority, which no one disputes.

He turned the paper over, as though there were

ever anything on the back of a certificate like that, thought long and hard and then said that things were slack at the yard, and that's the truth. And if they happen to notice that they've got on with a man less for three months, it might be risky for me. Besides that, they soon get fed up with paying wages to someone who's off sick, so you shouldn't even mention it to Mr Henri, as he would be very likely to say that General and Marine Shipbuilding isn't a hospital and even less a pension fund. But, Hamer said, if you're willing to go on unpaid sick leave then I would be willing to take the responsibility for it, without mentioning it inside.

'Inside' is Mr Henri's private office, where no one goes except Hamer and the chief engineer. Whenever an ordinary employee is summoned there, he comes back with a red face. After three visits or so he is usually dismissed.

'Mr Henri probably won't even notice that you're not there,' said Hamer.

That's quite possible. For when Hamer was on holiday last year, I, as senior clerk, had to go inside in his place to take down letters. And at that time I realised that Mr Henri didn't know my name. At first he called me Hamer, out of habit I expect, and after that he didn't call me anything at all.

I talked over Hamer's proposal with my wife and we agree that it's a perfect solution in all respects. And by accepting his offer, I'll be proving yet again that I don't want to soil my hands with unearned wages.

Hamer put my certificate away so as to be able to justify himself, should word of it reach Mr Henri, and I didn't even have to say goodbye to my colleagues, as they're expecting me back, aren't they? Hamer really thinks I'll be back, at least if I get better. The dear man doesn't realise that he's been taken for a ride and is playing an active part in consolidating my fortune. I've firmly resolved to make it up to him later with a nice present.

And now the cheese world is mine for the taking.

## 8

Arranging his office is to a businessman what preparing baby clothes is to a young expectant mother.

I remember very well the birth of my first child, and I can still remember how my wife, after a full day's work, would sit under the lamp sewing until late at night, resting now and again till the pain in her back subsided. There was something solemn about it, like someone who's all alone in the world and goes on their way deaf and blind to everything else. I had a similar feeling as my first cheese day dawned.

I was up early, so early that my wife said I was mad. 'New brooms sweep clean,' she says.

First I have to decide whether to set up my office at home or in town.

My wife thinks home is best, because it's cheaper, as I won't have to pay extra rent and, what's more, my family can have the use of the telephone.

We inspected the house and decided on a small

room above the kitchen. It's next to the bathroom, so if you want a bath you have to go through my office, sometimes in your pyjamas, but that usually happens on Saturday afternoons or Sundays when my office has lost its official character. It's neutral territory then and as far as I'm concerned they can embroider or play cards in there, provided that they don't touch my files, because I won't put up with that.

The room is papered with landscapes depicting hunting and fishing trips, and at first I intended to have it repapered. An austere, plain background without flowers or anything, with nothing else hanging up except a tear-off calendar and, for instance, a map of the Dutch cheese area. Recently I saw a strikingly coloured map of the wine region around Bordeaux. There may be something similar for cheese production. But my wife felt that repapering could wait till my business had expanded a bit. 'Till things get moving,' she said finally. So I decided I might as well leave the old paper up for the time being.

Still, it would be better if I were to have my way, for who's at the helm of the cheese ship, my wife or me?

Later on, that wallpaper will have to go, as in the depths of my soul it's been condemned. And a businessman must follow his intuition, even if it means turning the whole world upside down.

I've got to see to headed stationery, a pedestal desk, a typewriter, a telegraphic address, letter files and a lot of other things, so I'm rushed off my feet. For it's all got to be done fast, seeing that the twenty tons of Edam will be starting its journey south in about three days' time. And everything will have to be shipshape by the time they arrive. The telephone must be ringing, the typewriter rattling and the files opening and closing. And I, as the brains behind the operation, must be at the centre of things.

I spent half a day racking my brains over the question of a letterhead. I feel it should have a modern company name rather than simply 'Frans Laarmans'. I'd also rather that word of my cheese venture didn't reach Mr Henri until I'm sure I'll never be setting foot inside General Marine again, except to deliver cheese to the canteen.

I would never have imagined that choosing a business name was so difficult. And yet millions of people who are less bright than I am have crossed that hurdle.

Whenever I see the name of an existing company, it always strikes me as perfectly normal, I'd even say familiar. The people couldn't have any name other than the one they have. But where was I to get a new name from? I was faced with all the problems of creation, because I had to conjure up a new name out of nothing.

I began quite simply with 'Cheese Merchant'.

But without my name underneath, it will be too imprecise. Cheese Merchant, Verdussenstraat 170,

Antwerp, looks suspicious, as though something is being kept hidden, as though there are worms in the cheese.

Then I came up with 'General Cheese Merchants'.

That was already an improvement. But a Flemish name like that is so naked, so unadorned. And I don't like 'cheese', as I've already said.

Next I tried COMMERCE GÉNÉRAL DE FROMAGE.

Sounds better, and 'Fromage' is less cheesy than 'Cheese'.

COMMERCE GÉNÉRAL DE FROMAGE HOLLANDAIS is another step forward. That will help keep away lots of people who need Gruyère or Cheshire, while I only deal in Edam. But 'Commerce' still isn't ideal.

ENTREPRISE GÉNÉRALE DE FROMAGE HOLLANDAIS.

That has a nice ring to it. But 'Entreprise' actually means *undertaking* and I'm not actually undertaking anything. Just storing cheese and selling it.

So ENTREPÔTS GÉNÉRAUX DE FROMAGE HOLLANDAIS.

But storage is secondary. And anyway I don't do it myself, as I don't want all that cheese at home. The neighbours would be up in arms and that's what haulage companies are for.

The selling is the main thing and what characterises my business. Turnover, as Hornstra says.

What the English call 'trading'. Wonderful word!

Why not go for an English company name, like the late-lamented General and Marine Shipbuilding

Company? England has a well-deserved worldwide reputation in trading matters.

GENERAL CHEESE TRADING COMPANY? I'm beginning to see the light. I feel I'm getting warmer.

What about ANTWERP CHEESE TRADING COMPANY? Or perhaps GENERAL EDAM TRADING COMPANY?

It won't do, so long as it's got cheese in it. It's got to be replaced by something else: foodstuffs, dairy products or something of the kind.

GENERAL ANTWERP FEEDING PRODUCTS ASSOCIATION?

Eureka! It makes the acronym Gafpa, nice and punchy. Best buy your cheese from Gafpa, sir! I can see you're not used to real Gafpa cheese, madam. Gafpa cheese melts in the mouth like honey. Hurry, our latest consignment of Gafpa cheese is nearly sold out. Later on, we'll be able to drop the cheese bit altogether, as Gafpa will have become synonymous with full-cream Edam cheese. I had just a roll and some Gafpa for lunch. That's what I must aim for.

And no one will know that good old Frans Laarmans is behind it all, except my family, my brother and my friend Van Schoonbeke, whom I told about my company name straightaway on the telephone, as the telephone is working and is of course a huge success.

My son Jan is calling all his schoolfriends, just for fun, and I have to wait my turn. I'll overlook it for the first day, I don't want to be petty-minded. But Van

Schoonbeke didn't understand what I said. He thought I said Gaspard, because that's the name of his friend with the gold teeth. Anyway, I can tell him on Wednesday. So I just told him my telephone was working and gave him my number. He congratulated me, as he always does, and said that I must bring him a sample of my Edam. Of course I shall, and a present too. He and Hamer will both get a nice present, as soon as I have time.

It's a shame that Gafpa can't be my telex address too, as that name is already taken by the firm of Gaffels and Parels. I hesitated between cheeseman, cheeseround, cheesetrader, cheesetrust, Laarmacheese and cheeseFrans, as there is a maximum of twelve letters, but I didn't like any of them. Finally I just turned Gafpa round and got Apfag. I almost wasn't allowed to use that either, as Apfa, without a *g*, already exists. It belongs to the Association Professionelle des Fabricants d'Automobiles and so has nothing to do with cheese.

My headed stationery can now be printed and as soon as it's ready, I'll write a letter to Hornstra. Not to get him to speed up the consignment, as I'm nowhere near finished organising my office, but he must see my stationery.

My wife is pleased to see me so busy. She's always on the go herself, and can't stand slacking.

I can see she's happy.

54

When I'm in my office she never goes to the bath-room without a word of apology, because she has to pass through my department. For example, she says, 'We're out of soap again.' Or, 'I've just got to get some warm water to wash a pullover.'

I smile benevolently at her and say 'Go right ahead.' But I must admit that I respect her kitchen just as she respects my office.

I sometimes have the impulse to give her a little pinch as she passes, but my office is sacred.

She telephones too – the butcher's and suchlike. It was quite a job teaching her, as she had never done it and simply couldn't understand that all one had to do was dial those few numbers to talk to the butcher. But she doesn't give up easily, and now she's telephoning like a veteran. She does keep waving her arms about though, as if the butcher can see her.

When I see her at work, either in the kitchen or upstairs or in the cellar, lugging washing or buckets, I find it astonishing that such a simple soul should have spotted that annoying clause in my contract with Hornstra so quickly.

And I think it's a terrible shame that my old mother didn't live to see this. I should have liked to see her using the telephone.

# 9

I took a sample of my headed stationery along to the gathering at my friend Van Schoonbeke's and showed it to him downstairs in the hall when he let me in.

'Many congratulations,' he said again, putting it in his pocket.

I was given the same place as last time as if by right, and I'm sure that not one of the three grandees would ever dare to take my seat.

That evening's topic was Russia.

Deep in my heart I admire those barefooted beggars who are trying to build a new temple from a pile of rubble. It must be a far cry from trying to shift twenty tons of cheese. But as the Gafpa man I mustn't give in to sentiment and I'm determined to trample underfoot anything that gets in the way of my cheese.

One of the grandees maintained that people were dying in their millions over there, like flies in an empty house. And at that moment that nice chap Van

Schoonbeke showed my headed notepaper to his next-door neighbour, who was interested and asked what it meant.

'It's the notepaper of our friend Laarmans' latest enterprise,' Van Schoonbeke explained. 'Haven't you seen it about yet?'

The coward said that he hadn't yet seen it but had heard about it, and he passed the piece of paper on to his neighbour. And so it went round the table in triumph.

'Very interesting', 'looks splendid', 'yes of course, nothing beats foodstuffs', came the comments from opposite and beside me. Tutankhamun's mummy would scarcely have created a bigger stir.

'What those Russians need is a proper Gafpa,' said Van Schoonbeke.

'I'll drink a toast to the prosperity of the Gafpa,' declared an old lawyer, who, I believe, is worth less than he pretends. He is at the bottom of the heap now that I have shaken off my suspect position as 'shipyards inspector', and now seizes every possible opportunity to empty his glass. All he cares about is the wine, I think.

I passed the paper on without deigning to look at it and so it came back to the host, who placed it on the table in front of him.

'You're quite a one, Frans,' said Van Schoonbeke when I took my leave.

'By the way,' he confided to me, 'Van der Zijpen the solicitor has asked me to recommend his youngest son to you with an eye to a partnership. They've got money, believe me, lots of it, and they're very respectable.'

Does he expect me to share the fruits of my labour with the first person who comes along? I wouldn't dream of it. Recommending the young chap to General Marine to take over my job there would be a different matter.

'The cheese has arrived, Dad,' cried my son Jan, who was standing in the doorway when I got home.

The news was confirmed by my daughter.

Someone had phoned up to ask what they were supposed to do with it. But Ida had forgotten the name, or maybe not understood it. Why hadn't she called her mother? She had gone out to do some shopping.

Isn't it scandalous that there was twenty tons of cheese waiting for me in town and no one could tell me where it was? Nice that you can rely on your children. Was it really true? Was it some hoax of Van Schoonbeke's? Or had she perhaps misunderstood?

But Ida stuck to her story. She was like a mule. They had said that twenty tons of cheese had arrived and asked for instructions. They had also said something about hats.

I ask you. First it was cheese and now it's hats. Couldn't you just box the ears of a girl like that?

And the young madam is in her fourth year at grammar school.

I was too nervous to eat and went up to my office. If my wife had come to bring some soap or 'just to get some warm water', I'd have given her some water all right.

'No playing the piano now,' I heard her order downstairs. That sign of respect did me a power of good.

'It's as if you're having regrets,' my wife said curtly. 'You are waiting for the cheese, aren't you? It's got to come.'

'Regrets? What do you mean, regrets?' I snapped at her. 'But have you ever heard anything like it? The Edam That Vanished into Thin Air or The Cheese That Turned into Hats. It's like the title of a B-movie.'

'But don't get all worked up,' my wife said. 'If the cheese hasn't arrived then there's been a misunderstanding. And if it has arrived, all the better. The cheese won't go back to Holland, will it? All the offices are shut now, but I bet you'll hear from the railways first thing tomorrow. Or is the cheese coming by boat?'

I wasn't sure about that. How was I supposed to know? But the idiot that called up ought to know. 'Come on, Frans, best have something to eat and be patient till tomorrow. It's too late now anyway.'

So I sat down, with a last savage look at the ninny

in question, who was standing there with tears in her eyes, but with a determined line round her mouth. And on top of that she was furious, because a little while later when Jan, who's a year older, put his hat on her plate with a knife next to it, she gave the piece of headgear such a swipe that it landed in the kitchen under the stove.

Yes, yes. The cheese has arrived. I feel it in my bones.

# 10

The next morning I was rung up a little after nine by the Blue Hat Haulage Company to ask where they were to deliver the cheese.

Now I understand all about the hats. I'll give her a bar of chocolate.

I answered by asking what they usually did with Edam.

'Take them to the buyers. Just give us the addresses.'

I replied that the twenty tons were not sold yet.

'Then we can keep them in our patent store,' came the reply.

It's hard to think on the telephone, in my opinion. It all happens too quickly for me. And I didn't want to consult my wife. Giving her a say in whether or not my office is to be repapered is quite normal in my view, but when it comes to the fate of the cheese itself, then I must be the boss. I am the Gafpa, aren't I?

'It would be best if you dropped by our office,' was the advice.

That patronising invitation put my back up – it was as if they were taking me and my cheese under their wing. And I don't need anyone's protection, just like I don't need that solicitor's son with all his money.

Nevertheless I accepted the offer, not only to put an end to all the telephoning, but because I feel I must go to meet my cheese now that it has arrived in Antwerp. This consignment is the advance guard of an army with which I must become personally acquainted. And I wouldn't want Hornstra to find out later that his Edam was met with indifference on the first leg of its journey.

Before I reached the haulage company, the fate of my cheeses was already settled. I'm becoming more decisive by the day.

They must be put in store. What else am I supposed to do with them?

I don't think Van Schoonbeke told Hornstra that I was a clerk with General Marine and so not only had to get the hang of the cheese business, but had to get my office organised too. In any case I haven't been able to concentrate on the actual selling yet. I haven't even found a pedestal desk, or a typewriter.

That's my wife's fault too: she maintains that I can pick up a secondhand desk for a few hundred francs. In the office furniture shops a desk like that costs two thousand francs or so, but then you get it delivered the same afternoon and the matter's settled. And I don't think a purchase like that should take up more than half an hour, as time doesn't stand still and days can turn into weeks. And I have to get round to shifting the cheese sooner or later.

Into the store with it then.

But if those haulage people thought they were impressing me with their talk of 'patent store' then they've got it all wrong. Come, come. I'm not falling for that one, gentlemen!

I want to see the store with my own eyes. I want to be sure that my cheese will rest safe, fresh and undisturbed, free from rain and rats, as in a family grave.

So I inspected their store and I have to admit that it's all right. It's vaulted, the floor is dry and the walls did not echo when I knocked on them with a stick.

My cheese won't escape from here, of that I can rest assured. And quite a bit of cheese has been housed here, I can smell that. If Hornstra sees this store, I'll be congratulated.

My twenty tons were on four trailers in their yard, because they had unloaded the cheese the night before, otherwise the railway would have charged me storage costs. And so I was able to be present at the storing of my cheese in its own compartment. I stood in the middle of the store like a riding-school instructor, and kept an eye on everything till the last box had been brought in.

Hornstra's trial consignment consists of nearly ten thousand cheeses, each weighing approximately two kilos, packed in three hundred and seventy patent boxes. 'Edam is usually sent loose,' said the man, 'but this is top-class full-cream cheese and worth packing.' The packaging makes delivery easier, so I'll sell in multiples of twenty-seven cheeses, as there are twenty-seven cheeses in each box. The last box had been broken open. 'By customs,' said the haulage man. And they'd cut one of my cheeses in half. One half was missing and I asked where it had got to.

Whereupon the man asked if I had done much business at the port. He had the impression I was completely new to the trade, otherwise I would surely have known that with customs it was a matter of give and take.

'Don't you know, sir, that they had the right to open those three hundred and seventy boxes one by one? We could have got customs to refund the cost of the cheese that had been cut open, but I gave half to the customs clerk and saved Hornstra three thousand francs' duty, because the cheese was listed as half-fat, when it's actually full-fat, which carries a higher duty. You see what I'm getting at, sir?'

There was something threatening about the repetition of the word 'sir'.

Then he asked if he could deliver a box to my home, as I was bound to be needing samples.

I felt it was better not to get on the wrong side of the haulage company people and so I approved the delivery of the box to my house, even though I have no immediate need for samples. First my office has to be in perfect order. Then I'll start selling.

After giving the man the remaining half of the cut cheese as a tip – there's nothing I like better than the sight of someone smiling all over his face – I recommended my cheese to him warmly and then the door was closed, a door like that of a fortress in the time of the Crusades.

I can go home with a light heart. My Edams won't get out of here, or not by force at least. They'll lie here till the day of their resurrection, when they shall be taken out in triumph and sit in all their glory in shop windows like those I stood in front of on my return from Amsterdam.

# 11

When I got home the case was already in my office. A heavy case containing twenty-six cheeses, each weighing two kilos, plus packaging. Sixty kilos all told.

Why hadn't he put the case in the cellar? It was in the way here and the smell of cheese was already penetrating through the planks. I tried shifting it, but couldn't.

The only thing for it was to get a crowbar.

And then I started hammering until the house shook and my wife came upstairs to see if she could help me. She told me that Mrs Peeters, who lives next to us and suffers from biliousness, had stood in her doorway and watched till the case was inside and the haulage company man had left the street with his cart. I said that Mrs Peeters could drop dead for all I cared, and after taking a break I managed to get one plank loose. I don't exactly know what's patent about

them but they are certainly sturdy cases. The rest
was child's play, and after one last effort they
appeared. Cheese after cheese wrapped in silver
paper, looking like huge Easter eggs. I myself had
already seen them at the warehouse, but I still found
it affecting.

The cheese fantasy had become reality.

I stated firmly that they had to go into the cellar
and my wife agreed, because cheese dries out.

She called Jan and Ida and the four of us went
downstairs carrying two cheeses each, so we completed the transfer in three trips. The last two cheeses
were fetched by the children. I was going to take the
big empty case downstairs myself, but Jan, who is
going on sixteen and is quite a sportsman, took it
from me, put it on his head and took it down to the
cellar like that. On the way down he kept letting go
with his hands, like a balancing act.

Downstairs my wife put the twenty-six Edam
cheeses back in the case and I covered them up by
laying the planks of the lid loosely on top of them.

'And now you must try the cheese,' I said, having
taken charge once and for all.

Whereupon Jan grabbed one of the silver balls,
threw it in the air, let it roll along his arm to his
chin and only gave it to my wife when he saw the
look I was giving him. Ida, who also wanted to do
her bit, carefully removed its silver wrapper and sure

enough a red cheese emerged, like the ones I have known since childhood and which are on sale all over town.

After we had stood looking at it for a moment, poker-faced, I gave the order to cut it in half.

First my wife tried, then Ida got the knife halfway in, and Jan did the rest.

My wife sniffed it first, then cut off a slice, tasted it and gave each of the children a piece. I officiated.

'Don't you want to try a bit?' my wife finally asked, having swallowed a couple of pieces. 'It's really tasty.'

I don't like cheese, but what else could I do? Shouldn't I set an example from now on? Shouldn't I lead the army of cheese-eaters from the front? So I managed to get a piece down, then telephoned my brother.

He put his bike in the hall, as he does every day, and his cheerful steps echoed through the house.

'I'm not intruding, I hope,' he asked, when he was already in the kitchen. 'Is that your cheese then, lad?'

And without further ado he cut a piece off and took a big bite.

I followed the impression it made from his animated features. At first he knitted his brows, as though he could taste something suspicious, and looked at my wife, who was still licking her lips.

'Magnificent,' he pronounced suddenly. 'I've never in my life tasted such splendid cheese.'

If it's true I needn't worry, because he's sixty-two and has always eaten cheese.

If only my office were finished.

'And have you sold much yet?' he enquired, cutting off another piece.

I said that I would only be starting when everything was perfectly organised.

'Well, get a move on with organising it,' he advised. 'Because if those twenty tons are intended as a trial, then those people may be expecting you to sell ten tons or so a week. Don't forget that you're the agent for the whole country. And then there's the Grand Duchy as well. If I were you I'd take the plunge and get moving straightaway.'

And with that he was gone, leaving me alone with my wife and children, and the cheese.

In the evening I went to Van Schoonbeke's to type a letter to Hornstra on Gafpa paper, as I still haven't got a typewriter and I must acknowledge the safe receipt of the consignment. I took the opportunity of bringing half an Edam cheese for van Schoonbeke, as he sets great store by such marks of appreciation. After tasting it he congratulated me yet again and said that he would save my cheese to serve to his friends at the next gathering. If I agree he will also ensure that I am a candidate in the forthcoming presidential election of the Association of Belgian Cheese Merchants. And now to work.

## 12

I've spent all week hunting high and low for a second-hand desk and ditto typewriter. And I assure you that trudging round all those secondhand shops in the old part of town is no picnic.

They are usually so full of junk that I can't possibly tell from the street whether they've got what I'm looking for in stock and I'm forced to go inside and ask. I don't mind that chore, it's just that I can't leave a shop without buying something, or a pub without having a drink.

So to start with I bought a carafe, a penknife and a plaster Saint Joseph. I can use the penknife, though I rather dislike it, and I took the carafe home, where it caused quite a stir. I left the statue of Saint Joseph on a windowsill a few streets further on when there was no one in sight, and made myself scarce. Because after the carafe I swore never to take anything else home and I couldn't go on walking around with that plaster statue.

But now I stand in the doorway and ask from there whether they've got a pedestal desk and a typewriter for sale. As long as I'm still holding the door handle I'm not really in the shop and so have no moral obligation, because I'm fed up with all that buying. But if the door isn't shut the bell goes on ringing and if that goes on too long you stand there like a thief wondering whether to pounce or not.

To make matters worse I'm never entirely easy about walking through town. Hamer may have my certificate, but someone who's seriously ill stays at home and doesn't go round the shops. I'm always frightened of bumping into people from General Marine, because I don't know how a real neurotic behaves. If I collapse they'll throw water in my face, give me smelling salts or take me to a doctor or chemist, whose verdict will be that I'm pretending. No, I don't want that, thanks very much. It's better if they don't see me. So I keep my eyes open and I'm ready to do an about-turn, or dodge into a side street. All things considered it would be best if my absence continues without there being too much talk about it.

Though I wouldn't mind knowing how things are at the yard.

It's quarter past nine. I know that my four fellow

clerks are in front of their typewriters at this moment, with their calves against the heating pipe, like gunners at their artillery pieces. One of the four is telling a joke. Yes, that first half-hour was fun. Hamer has opened his ledger without warming himself first and the telephone operator runs her hand lightly over her blonde hair, which she had permed just before I left. The clanking of the pneumatic riveting hammers in the yard penetrates our office and outside our busy miniature locomotive passes our windows. We turn our five heads and wave at old Piet in his blue overalls and neckerchief, who drives it as sedately as a coachman drives his old nag. He returns our greeting by giving a short blast on his steam whistle. And in the distance our high chimney flutters its black flag of smoke.

The poor suckers are standing there now, while I am busy hacking my way through the jungle of the business world.

Seek and ye shall find, and I've just experienced the truth of that. Because I've finally found a suitable desk, with only a couple of moth holes in the green baize top. It's three hundred francs and even though it's not new it will serve just as well as one costing two thousand. So my wife was right. But this has taken another week and my cheese is waiting impatiently for the cellar to be opened.

The problem of the typewriter has also been

solved. I discovered that they can be hired, and tomorrow I'm having one delivered that I'm familiar with, namely a sister machine of the Underwood that I earned my living on for thirty years.

Last Wednesday the selling cycle began – at Van Schoonbeke's, in fact, who himself is pleased that things are going so well.

Once all his friends were in their places he opened a cupboard and put the remainder of the half-Edam on the table. I could see that he had already eaten a fair amount of it.

'One of the specialities of our friend Laarmans,' he said by way of introduction.

'Excuse me, of Gafpa,' said the old lawyer. 'Are we allowed a taste?'

And he immediately cut off a piece and passed the plate on.

I liked the way the man wouldn't stand for any slight against Gafpa. If all goes well he'll get a cheese as a present.

A little while later the whole ensemble was chewing away and I sincerely believe that no kind of cheese ever received such enthusiastic praise as this full-fat Edam. From all sides there were exclamations of 'Wonderful!' 'Superb!' 'Fanstastic!' and the chic fellow asked where the cheese could be obtained.

So my prestige was already so great that they didn't even dare ask me personally.

'The floor is yours, Mr Laarmans,' announced my friend, popping another piece into his mouth.

'Of course,' said someone else, 'only Mr Laarmans himself can give us the information.'

'Do you imagine that Mr Laarmans concerns himself with such trifles?' said the old gentleman. 'You must understand. If I want that cheese, I'll ring up Gafpa.'

'And say you'd like fifty grams delivered,' added his neighbour.

I now announced casually that Gafpa only delivered orders of twelve cases of twenty-seven cheeses or more, but that nevertheless I was prepared to supply this full-fat cheese retail at wholesale price.

'Three cheers for our friend Laarmans,' cried the old man. And he emptied his glass once again.

They know my name now.

Then I took out my new fountain pen and noted down the orders. Each of them will get a two-kilo cheese. As we were leaving the old gentleman asked, as we were putting on our coats together, if he mightn't have half a cheese as an exception since he lived alone with his sister and a maid. And I promised him he could, because he was the first to think of the Gafpa.

One of them asked what Gafpa's other specialities were.

'You're trying to tell me that Gafpa sells nothing but cheese? Come, come, stop pulling my leg.'

I admitted that cheese was just a sideline, but said that for the time being the other items could only be supplied to shops.

# 13

I am beginning to realise that time is money, because I wasted a whole morning delivering those seven and a half cheeses.

I discovered a wicker suitcase in the loft that can take three Edam cheeses and I delivered them myself, because my children have lots of homework after school and my boy would be juggling with the cheeses en route.

When my wife saw me going down to the cellar with that case, I had to tell her what was going on. I was trying do it quietly, because I was afraid she would find it all comical. After all, lugging cheeses about is not really a job for the director of a business, but I can't have my ten thousand cheeses delivered one by one by the Blue Hat Haulage Company. They won't do that. But my wife thought it was quite normal.

'That's a start,' she said. 'And at least they'll get to know our cheese that way.'

That 'our' did me good. It means she is participating and taking her share of responsibility.

I hope they don't reorder, because the deliveries were harder than I thought. First I had to keep a straight face as I passed Mrs Peeters, our neighbour, who is always standing in the doorway, or at the window. Then I boarded the tram, where the case got in the way. When you get to a house you ring, a maid opens the door and there you stand in the hall with your basket, because it's more like a basket than a case. You have to say that you've brought the cheese, whereupon the maid goes to tell Madame, who is sometimes still in bed. In two cases out of eight they knew nothing about cheese and I had the greatest difficulty getting rid of those heavy rounds, which I was only able to do by saying that there was nothing to pay. I would settle up with Monsieur.

And now I'm sitting in my office after that exhausting expedition and after another visit to my brother, who asks every day about the figures for sold and unsold cheese. Like a real doctor he keeps on putting the knife in the wound.

I told him about the cheese that was sold at van Schoonbeke's. He was very gratified that they all found them so delicious. But then he made a brief calculation and said, 'That's seven and a half of your ten thousand. If you do a deal like that every week, it'll be thirty years before you sell the last cheeses. Get to work, lad, get to work, or it'll end badly.'

But how can I get rid of all that cheese? That is the question.

For a moment I had the idea of visiting every shop in town that sells cheese with a couple of Edams in my suitcase. But if I used that system my office would be left unmanned and become redundant. And I'm indispensable for correspondence and bookkeeping, I reckon. Besides, I can't leave my wife to talk to anyone who might phone up. She's got enough work as it is.

No, my cheese must be sold by a team of alert agents. Chaps who penetrate even the smallest shops, have the gift of the gab, and bring in their orders every week, or even twice a week. Yes, twice a week would be better and I'll make Monday and Thursday the days – that will help to spread my own workload a bit. I'll enter everything properly myself, give the haulage company instructions about delivery, make out the invoices, see to collection of the money, deduct my five per cent and send the balance to Hornstra every week. And I wouldn't even have to have any contact with the cheese myself.

So I placed an ad:

Wholesale Edam cheese importer seeks competent representatives in every town in Belgium and in the Grand Duchy of Luxembourg, preferably with experience of dealing with cheese shops. Write to Gafpa, Verdussenstraat 170, Antwerp, giving references and details of previous employment.

It had the desired effect.

Two days later I received a hundred and sixty-four letters of every size and colour. The postman had had to ring the doorbell because he couldn't get them in the letterbox.

So I'm heading in the right direction and at least I'll have a use for my typewriter.

First I'll have to open all those letters and sort them into provinces, then I'll buy a map of Belgium and pin a flag on every town where I've appointed an agent. That will give me a splendid overview. And those who don't sell enough will have to go.

Brussels is top with seventy letters. Then comes Antwerp with thirty-two, and the rest are spread over the whole country. Only the Grand Duchy has produced no replies, but that is a minor matter.

After everything had been opened and classified, an extra fifty or so arrived that must have been posted late. Things are going well. I have started with Brussels. There are people who tell their life's history, from childhood on. Many begin by saying that they served in the Great War and won seven combat medals. I can't see what that has to do with selling cheese. Others go on about their large families and the rotten times they've been through and appeal to the goodness of my heart. Reading some of the letters brought tears to my eyes. I shall put them away in a special place because I don't want them to be seen by my children, or else they'll go on about it till I give those people special treatment. And I have to plough through them all. If I answer all the letters it is purely out of politeness and also to have a chance to bang away at my typewriter, because many of these people have never been in business, once sold cigarettes or have just written for the hell of it. Those who meet the requirements write confidently and ask for information on rates of commission and fixed salary. They seem to want to have a good think about whether they'll do me the pleasure of accepting one of my agencies.

Of course I have no intention of paying any of these blokes a salary. Where would it end? They'll get three per cent and not a penny more. I'll be left with two per cent, plus my three hundred guilders a month.

I had just settled in front of my Underwood when there was a ring at the door. I can hear it from here, but pay it no attention, as I never open the door myself when I'm in the office. But a little while later my wife came upstairs and said there were a gentleman and three ladies who wanted to talk to me. They had a parcel with them.

'Put your collar and tie on,' she advised.

Who could they be? I decided they must be candidates who preferred coming in person to writing.

As I opened the door of our sitting room, four outstretched hands were thrust at me. It was Tuil, Erfurt, Bartherotte and Miss Van der Tak, my four fellow clerks at General Marine.

I could feel the blood draining from my face and they must have noticed something, as Anna van der Tak pushed a chair towards me and told me to sit down.

'You mustn't tire yourself. We'll be off in a moment,' she reassured me.

They had decided to come and visit me to see for themselves how I was getting on, as the craziest rumours were circulating.

Tuil apologised for their having come at lunchtime, but I knew they had no time during the day. And it was out of the question to visit someone who was ill in the evening.

They kept looking at me and exchanging understanding glances.

A lot had changed at the office in those few weeks. They were now seated with their backs to the window instead of the other way round, they had all been given a new roll of blotting paper, and Hamer was wearing glasses.

'Just imagine Hamer with glasses,' said Erfurt. 'It's hysterical.'

While they were talking I heard my brother coming in. He put his bike against the wall and marched towards the kitchen as he does every afternoon. His martial step reverberated through the hallway.

I was afraid he would ask me from out there how cheese sales were going, because he bellows like a ship's captain, out of pure enthusiasm. But my wife must have signalled to him to keep quiet, because a little while later I heard him tiptoeing out.

Next Tuil made a short speech on behalf of the whole staff and expressed the hope that I would soon be as right as rain and take up my place among them once again.

And with a solemn gesture Bartherotte suddenly produced a large parcel from behind his back and handed it to me, asking me to open it.

It was a beautifully polished backgammon set, with fifteen black and fifteen white counters, two leather cups and two dice. There was silver plate on the lid of the box, with the inscription:

FROM THE STAFF OF THE
GENERAL MARINE AND SHIPBUILDING COMPANY
TO THEIR COLLEAGUE
FRANS LAARMANS
ANTWERP, 15 FEBRUARY 1933.

They had taken up a collection and even old Piet, the engine driver, had chipped in with his franc.

And after a last cordial handshake they left.

The backgammon set is for me to play on with my wife and children until I have recovered.

My wife said nothing. She is cooking the dinner with a worried look on her face. I sense that one harsh word could make her cry.

# 14

A fortnight ago I appointed thirty agents, spread all over the country, without a fixed salary, but with a sizeable commission. And still no orders are coming in. What are those people doing? They're not even writing to me and my brother goes on imperturbably enquiring about the quantities sold.

I had to choose those agents on sight, as one buys cattle at market. I called them to my office in batches of ten, one a little later than the other, so as to avoid embarrassing encounters between rivals. You don't make starving dogs eat from the same bowl.

Mrs Peeters, my neighbour, must have had a busy time of it.

It was a surprise from start to finish.

People who had written splendid letters sometimes turned out to be wrecks. They were big, small, old, young, with and without children, smartly dressed and in rags, imploring and threatening. They talked about their rich families, ex-government ministers they knew. And it gave me a peculiar sensation sitting there, knowing that I could turn one of those ecstatic fellows into a heap of rags with a single word.

One man said frankly that he was hungry and would be content with a cheese, even without an agency. I was so moved that I gave him an Edam. Afterwards I heard that on his way out he had managed to wangle a pair of my old shoes out of my wife.

It was hard to get some of them to leave because it was so nice and warm in my office. And two declared that it wasn't acceptable to get someone to come to Antwerp without paying his expenses. So I thought I might as well reimburse them. In each case I noted down on their letter: bad, doubtful, good, bald, a drinker, has walking stick and suchlike, because after the tenth caller I could no longer remember the first few.

I seriously considered whether I should not take care of Antwerp myself after all. That would mean that Frans Laarmans would be the Gafpa agent here in town. But the vision of my deserted office plays on my mind. What would the public think of the Gafpa if they could not even get an answer on the telephone?

At that moment my youngest brother-in-law came and asked if he could have a go at Antwerp. He's really a diamond polisher, but because things are so slack he's been out of work for months.

'Delfine said I should talk to you about it,' he declared with the false subservience of someone who knows he has protection from on high.

I went to the kitchen to talk to 'Delfine' and get confirmation. And she simply said that he came every day and went on about the cheese. This time she doesn't have the last word, the way she did in the discussion about whether or not to repaper my office.

'Should I entrust Antwerp to Gust or not?' I asked her in a businesslike tone, looking closely at her.

In reply she mumbled something, of which I didn't understand a word, grabbed a washtub and went down to the cellar.

What else could I do but take him on for a trial period? But if it doesn't work then out he must go, brother-in-law or no brother-in-law. It'll cost me at least a whole cheese that I'll never see again.

I have had order slips printed. They are divided into columns showing the date of order, name and address of the purchaser, number of boxes of twenty-seven cheeses of approx. two kilograms each, price per kilo, and payment terms. There is room for fifteen orders on each slip. To start with, each agent has received ten slips, that is, enough for five weeks. I've kept it as simple and practical as possible. All they have to do is fill their slips in every Monday and

Thursday and post them to me. The rest follows automatically.

However, since there was no sign of any orders, I finally paid a visit to my two Brussels agents, Noeninckx and Delaforge, to find out what was wrong and, if necessary, to lend them my support. You see, I had divided Brussels into an eastern and a western half, since I felt the city was too large to be covered adequately by one man.

After an interminable tram ride, I was told that Noeninckx was completely unknown at the address given. But in that case how did my letters get through to him? They certainly weren't returned to me.

Delaforge lives in a totally different neighbourhood, in a loft I think, as the stairs did not go any higher. There was washing hanging out to dry on the landing and a smell of fried herring. I knocked at his door for quite a while, until he finally opened up in his shirt-sleeves, his eyes still puffy with sleep. He did not even recognise me and when I told him who I was, he told me he wasn't interested in the cheese business. Whereupon he slammed the door in my face.

I'm mystified.

## 15

Being beset by worries, I was in a listless mood during my weekly visit to Van Schoonbeke and his friends. And I had only shaken hands with half of them before he congratulated me again. I looked at him reproachfully, because I find these periodic congratulations without reason humiliating and I won't be messed around. But he briefly explained the situation to his friends – and hence to me.

'Our friend Laarmans has been elected president of the Association of Belgian Cheese Merchants. Here's to his great success,' he declared.

They all emptied their glasses, because they are always ready to drink to anything at all with van Schoonbeke's wine.

'That young man will go a long way,' said the one with the gold teeth.

I protested, since it must be a lame joke of our host's, but the old lawyer with the half-cheese declared that a self-made man like me must throw off humility like a worn-out coat. Raise the cheese banner aloft, my good sir!

On my way out I asked Van Schoonbeke why he had played that joke on me, but he insisted that it was all wrapped up and gave me a benevolent smile, since he means well.

'President!' he intoned admiringly.

Of course he considers it a gain in prestige, not only for me but also indirectly for himself and all his friends. I would be the second president, as one of the others is president of the Antwerp Association of Grain Importers.

I can't understand it, because I didn't ask for anything and don't even know the association, though I'm a member.

The next morning's mail brought the explanation in the form of a letter from the Association Professionelle des Négociants en Fromage, informing me that I been elected vice-president. Even being a deputy is too much for me. I don't want to be a vice-president. I want my brother to hold his tongue, my office to work efficiently, and my agents to sell. And people not to interfere. The letter also gave the reason. Three years ago the import duty on cheese have been raised to twenty per cent of market value and ever since, led by their chairman, they had been trying in vain to have the duty lowered again. This Friday, which was tomorrow, they were due to have another audience at the Department of Trade and were adamant that I should lead their delegation.

Their letter greatly alarmed me, since the name of a vice-president of such a professional association is bound to receive some publicity, that I do know. It can't be avoided. No way of avoiding it. And even for all the money in the world I don't want Hamer and the whole staff of General Marine crowding round a newspaper in a day or two that contains my photograph as the Belgian cheese supremo. I can't have that. I can't risk that.

I'll go to Brussels tomorrow and tell the gentlemen that my health won't permit it. And if they won't listen I'll resign my membership and their association can go to hell. I'm sorry for Van Schoonbeke, but there's nothing else I can do.


In the Palace Hotel I found four cheese people who introduced themselves as Hellemans from Brussels, Dupierreux from Liège, Bruaene from Bruges and a fourth chap from Ghent whose name I didn't catch. And as time was short we had to get moving.

'Gentlemen, please excuse me, but I cannot accept,' I said. 'Elect someone else,' I implored them. 'I'd really appreciate it if you did.'

But they would not relent and we could not go back, as the Director-General, or maybe even the minister himself, was expecting us at ten o'clock and our five names had been given. They had not expected any resistance – on the contrary, since that lawyer chap from Antwerp had said that I would like nothing better. So that was it. Once again the work of my dreadful friend who wants me to get on in the world.

'Listen,' said Dupierreux, who was getting nervous, 'if you don't want to be vice-president, at least go through this one formality with us. In an hour's time you'll be an ex-vice-president.'

On that condition I finally agreed and went along with them.

After we had sat in the waiting room for a while with a delegation of brewers, a messenger appeared, called out, 'The Association Professionelle des Négociants en Fromage,' and led us into the office of Mr de Lovendegem de Pottelsberghe, the Director-General of the Department, who after a courteous welcome pointed us to five chairs in front of his desk.

'After you, Mr President,' said Hellemans. And after I had sat down they took their seats.

The Director-General adjusted his glasses and took out a particular dossier from a pile which he glanced at for a moment. Things were going quickly, which made me think that the main issue was already known to him. He kept shaking his head and shrugging his shoulders as though he was faced with an impossible task. Finally he sat back in his chair and looked at all of us, me in particular.

'Gentlemen,' he declared, 'I am terribly sorry, but it's impossible this year. It would make a hole in the current budget at an inopportune moment, not to mention the tremendous outcry among home producers, with a press campaign and the usual questions in parliament. But we'll review the situation next year.' At that moment his telephone rang.

'The pigeon breeders will have to wait till I've finished with the cheese merchants,' he snapped and rang off.

'But,' he continued consolingly, 'I promise I won't give in to our own producers who will be coming to insist on a new ten per cent rise.' And he looked at his watch.

My four adjutants looked in my direction and, since I said nothing, Dupierreux said that it was no surprise as they were told the same thing on every visit. There followed a confused discussion about domestic and foreign cheese varieties, with statistics I could make neither head nor tail of. Their four voices merged into a buzz that seemed to be fading into the background. And finally I found myself a few steps away, looking down at the quartet as they made their demands. There was Hellemans, an elderly man who had given the best years of his life to cheese, Bruaene, a heavily built chap, bursting with health and with a thick gold chain across his stomach, Dupierreux, a small, nervous type who found it hard to control himself, and finally the man from Ghent with his spotty hands, hunched forward with his elbows on his knees as though he didn't want to miss one syllable of what was said. All four of them respected names in cheese, people with a past, a cheese pedigree, people with authority, money. And into their midst had strayed Frans Laarmans who knew as much about cheese as about chemistry. What had these disgusting cheeseworms done to this poor man? Suddenly my chair slid backward, as though of its own accord. I stood up and, looking furiously at the four cheesified dolts, declared loudly that I had had enough.

They looked at me in astonishment, as people look at a first attack of madness.

I saw de Lovendegem de Pottelsberghe go pale. He braced himself, rounded his desk, came hurriedly up to me and put his white hand on my arm in a conciliatory gesture.

'Come, come, Mr Laarmans,' he said, attempting to calm me down, 'I didn't mean it like that. What do you say to a five per cent reduction and five per cent next year. Show a little flexibility now. I dare not take it upon myself to do it all in one go.'

'Agreed,' said the man from Ghent. And a little while later I was standing on the pavement, surrounded by my beaming comrades-in-cheese who all shook hands with me at once.

'Mr Laarmans,' mumbled Dupierreux with great emotion, 'we are so grateful. We never dared hope for anything like this. It's splendid.'

'And my vice-presidency is now over and done with, isn't it, gentlemen?'

'Of course it is,' said Bruaene reassuringly. 'We don't need you any more.'

# 16

A letter has arrived from Amsterdam in which Hornstra says he has to go to Paris on Tuesday and will take advantage of his journey through Belgium to settle up with me over those twenty tons. He will be here at eleven in the morning.

Was it from shame or rage? I don't know. But when I got the letter I went bright red, even though I was sitting alone and unseen in my office, which is now fully equipped.

I put the letter in my pocket, because I don't want my wife to know about it, or else she'll be bound to tell my brother. But one thing is certain. If those Edam cheeses are not sold in a day or two, Gafpa will have been torpedoed. In fact, I only have four days left, because Sundays don't count for businessmen.

With a heavy heart I fetched my wicker suitcase from the loft and stuffed one of my cheeses into it.

My wife will probably think that my friends have put in a second order.

Come on Frans, enough of all your claptrap about offices. You've got to get out there yourself, with only your tongue and the quality of your full-fat cheese to help you.

I know exactly where I must go. If they are going to sell anywhere, it will be there.

But what line should I take? Just ask if they want to buy some cheese?

Now I realise that I lack practice, because I have never sold anything. And now I've suddenly got to shift all that cheese. If only it were mimosa. Yet I'm only faced with an everyday problem. What do all those millions of businesspeople do? They need to sell too, don't they?

That complimentary copy of *Le Soir* is still lying on my desk. I open it to have another look at my advert. It looks so good that I'm tempted to apply myself and offer my services.

And my eye falls involuntarily on a little insert, just below mine: 'Written and face-to-face advice to businessmen and agents experiencing sales difficulties. Years of experience. Boorman, Villa des Roses, Brasschaet.'

That district is nearby. Why shouldn't I consult the chap before taking the decisive step?

And that's what I did, like a patient resorting to quacks without the knowledge of his doctor.

---

I had to wait my turn.

Boorman is a stocky old gentleman, with a large head and a fixed gaze, who sits with his back to the window and lets the bright daylight shine on his visitors.

He listened to my Gafpa story without interrupting me, and then said that there are two important things for me to learn: how I enter and what I say. First and foremost, how do you make your entrance? You can enter like someone with something to give or like someone asking for something, like a businessman or like a beggar. The beggar style, says Boorman, is less a matter of dress than of attitude and tone.

So you enter nonchalantly, maybe holding a cigar, throw your case down as though it contains anything in the world except cheese, and ask if you have the honour.

He of course says yes. And if you *don't* have the honour he does.

You sit down, if necessary uninvited.

'Sir, after taking soundings about your firm we've come specially from Amsterdam to offer you the Antwerp monopoly of our full-fat Gafpa cheese.'

*We* means that in fact a whole official committee has come, but the others are still at the hotel. Yesterday evening after we arrived we strolled around for a bit.

*Specially from Amsterdam* is an appeal to the goodness

of his heart, says Boorman. Because if he doesn't buy then all the committee can do is return to its home town and the whole trip will have been wasted. Moreover, confidence in his firm will have been shaken. And he should be sensitive to that, because *after taking soundings* implies that you have combed the whole of Antwerp and only he is left, and *our* full-fat cheese that the whole Dutch cheese industry is squarely behind you. He was prepared to give me practical lessons, but there's no time, because Hornstra is on his way.

That visit to Boorman was my last chance of reprieve. Abandoned by everyone, I must vanquish the cheese dragon on my own. I got past Mrs Peeters undetected with my case and took the tram to that cheese emporium with the splendid window display and the awful stink. First I stood in front of the window for a while, and looked for an Edam cheese among all the varieties. Yes, there's one, cut in half. Not a patch on my full-fat variety, I can tell at a glance.

The shop exudes the same smell as it did that evening. It's strange, but now I've been in the business for a while, I find it harder to bear than I did on my return from Amsterdam. Have I become softer? Or is it because of my mood?

The shop is thriving, that's for sure.

There are half a dozen customers inside and the shop girls are busy cutting, wrapping and handing over. Even from outside I can hear the repeated 'How can I help you, madam?'

I can't go charging in while all those customers are there and bring the whole business to a halt while I hold forth about my full-fat cheese. Because then it will turn into a lecture. But if I don't launch straight into it, then perhaps they'll ask, 'How can I help you, sir?' And the roles will be reversed.

The rush has subsided a bit. There is only one lady left.

Now or never.

But two of the shop girls, who have nothing to do, look at me, say something to each other, and start to laugh. The older one looks in the mirror for a moment and smoothes the creases out of her apron. Do they imagine perhaps that I'm going to come and chat them up?

I look at my watch, turn my back on them and, after waiting for a while, walk on a little further towards the Bass Tavern.

I go into the bar, as a policeman has also looked at me once or twice, and order a pale ale. I down the beer in a single draught and ask for a refill.

There's no question of going home without giving it a try, because I don't want to have to reproach myself with anything. A clear conscience is worth a lot. And they're not going to say that I let myself be seen off by those four vixens.

My second glass is empty. I glance at my wicker suitcase, grab it and head for the shop. A frontal attack.

As I pass the shop window I close my eyes for a second so as not to see how many customers there are. I'm going inside even if there are a hundred and I'll wait until I get a chance to say what I've got to say. I'll sit on my wicker suitcase in the meantime, if need be, because I've gone beyond shame.

The shop is empty. There are only the four girls in white behind the counter.

Which of the four should I address myself to? I don't think it's advisable to look from one to the other. That might throw me completely, because they might all answer at once.

I turn to the oldest one who was so coquettish just now and say that I've come specially from Amsterdam to offer Mr Platen the monopoly for Antwerp of our full-fat Edam cheese, at a price below all our competitors.

Platen was the name on the shop window. It hadn't escaped me.

As my sentence progresses I see her jaw dropping wider and wider, and when I get to the end, she asks, 'I beg your pardon, sir?'

Funny, but when you come to sell, people don't understand you.

Then I ask if she would call the manager, as I can

see I'm not going to make any headway with that foursome. Just to prove the point, three customers suddenly appear and shortly afterwards another two. And off it goes again: 'How can I help you, madam?'

They leave me there among great pats of butter, baskets full of eggs and stacks of ham. Yes, the customer is king, there's no getting away from it.

The till keeps tinkling, and each time I hear the bleating sound of 'Thank you, madam'.

I suddenly ask if Mr Platen is in, whereupon I am invited to look in the office behind the shop.

I edge cautiously past the butter and peer through a glass door. Sure enough, someone is sitting there. I knock and Platen – it is the man himself – calls out, 'Come in.'

His office can't hold a candle to mine. It's half an office and half a sitting room. There is even a gas stove. How the man can work here is beyond me. I ask you, are these fitting surroundings for a businessman? But there are enough papers and he seems to be busy. He is talking on the telephone in his shirtsleeves, without a collar or tie.

With a glance he enquires what I want, without putting down the receiver. I signal to him that I don't mind if he finishes his call and then he asks the purpose of my visit, as he has to go into town and has no time.

I repeat what I said back in the shop, calmly, striking something of an attitude with my bearing and voice. I have crossed my legs.

He looks at me and says, 'Five tons.'

I stood there in a daze, and was grabbing for my fountain pen when he repeated into the telephone, 'I can do you five tons at fourteen francs a kilo.' Then he rang off, got up and started putting on his collar.

'Who are you working for?' asked Platen, to which I replied, 'Hornstra.'

'I'm a cheese wholesaler myself. I know Hornstra well. For years I was his agent for Belgium and the Grand Duchy of Luxembourg, but in the end he got too expensive. So don't waste your time, sir.'

So he had had the Grand Duchy too.

'Can I take you anywhere?' he asked. 'If you have to go into town you can have a lift in my car.'

And I did, simply because it was the best way of getting through the shop under the gaze of the four girls.

I stayed in his car until he stopped in front of a smaller cheese shop and got out himself. If he had been driving to Berlin, I would have gone with him.

I thanked him, picked up my wicker suitcase and took the tram home.

My battery is empty. I have bled dry.

# 17

At home a further surprise was in store for me, because when Jan got back from school he called up that he had sold some cheese.

'A whole case,' he maintained.

And when I picked up the newspaper as if I hadn't heard, he went over to the telephone, dialled a number and started a conversation with one of his chums. First he made some joke in English and then I heard him ask his friend to call his father to the telephone. 'And be quick about it or you'll get a left uppercut from me tomorrow.'

And a little later he called out, 'Dad! Dad!'

He was right.

I found myself talking to a friendly stranger who said he was delighted to make the acquaintance of Jan's father and confirmed that I could deliver a case of twenty-seven cheeses.

'I've sold a case, uncle!' cried Jan when my brother came in.

'Well done, lad. But your main job is to swot up your Greek and Latin. Father will look after the cheese.'

I went ahead and sold that case, to oblige the father of Jan's friend. I took the cheese round myself in a taxi.

In the evening Jan and Ida had a fight.

He's making fun of her because she hasn't sold anything yet. He sings, 'cheese, cheese, cheese, cheese' in the ascending scale of 'do re mi fa' and when she finally flies at him, he keeps her at a distance with his long arms so as not to get kicked. She finally bursts into tears and confesses that she doesn't dare talk about cheese at school any more, because they've started to call her 'the cheese maid'.

So *she* had tried too.

I send Jan into the garden and give her a kiss.

# 18

I'm incapable of working and have lived through the last four days as if in a dream. Do you suppose I'm really falling ill now?

I've just been visited by that son of Van der Zijpen the solicitor, whom Van Schoonbeke had talked about.

He's a distinguished young chap of about twenty-five, who smells strongly of tobacco and can't stand or sit still for a minute without trying out a dance step.

'Mr Laarmans,' he said, 'I know you're a friend of Albert van Schoonbeke, and hence a gentleman. I'm counting on your discretion.'

What was I supposed to reply to that, especially in a mood like mine? So I just nodded briefly.

'My father is prepared to buy a partnership in your Gafpa business. I reckon we can take him for two hundred thousand little ones, perhaps more.'

He paused to offer me a cigarette, lit one up himself and looked at me as if to see what impression his preamble had made on me.

'And what then, sir?' I asked him coolly, because I did not like the sound of 'little ones' and 'take for'.

'Well, *then* it's very simple,' he said impudently. 'I become your partner, for a fixed monthly sum of four thousand francs. You take out four thousand francs a month too, obviously. But I have absolutely no aptitude for business and I certainly don't intend to drag out my days here. So I propose that you give me only three thousand each month and I sign receipts for four thousand, on condition that I don't have to set foot in your office, not even to get my money. I'll tell you where you can deliver it. At any rate we'll be able to get through a couple of years with that two hundred thousand and when that's gone we can see what happens. Perhaps we'll decide to inject some more capital. As far as my share of the profits is concerned, I make you a present of it. Isn't that a splendid offer?'

I told him that I would have to think it over and that I would let him know via Van Schoonbeke.

When he had gone I took off the wall my festively flagged map of Belgium, on which the cheese area of the local agent was marked out around each flag, and put it away.

Should I write another letter to my agents?

---

Come on, let's get it over with. It's time the cheese misery came to an end.

I had a thousand sheets of Gafpa headed notepaper. I cut off the blank bits. They may come in handy for Jan and Ida. The other bits are for the toilet.

Then I went down to the cellar.

There are still fifteen and a half cheeses in the case. Let's just check: one stayed with the customs and Blue Hat, a second was shared between Van Schoonbeke and myself; seven and a half rounds went to Van Schoonbeke's friends, I gave one to that cadging agent and one to my brother-in-law. Twenty-seven minus eleven and a half. That's right. Hornstra won't be able to complain about my meticulousness.

That half-round is bothering me. Anyway, why did that old fellow have to take only a half round? I pick up the piece and stand there dithering. I can return whole rounds, but not half-rounds. It would be a waste to throw it away.

I hear my wife going upstairs – to make the beds, I expect. I wait until she's upstairs, then creep quietly into the kitchen and lay the red half-moon on a board, round side up. To stop it drying out. Then I go back to the cellar, count the Edams once again and nail the case shut. I hammer as carefully as possible so as not to alarm my wife upstairs. She might think I was hanging myself.

Right, that's that. Now to the office to phone for a taxi, which arrives at the door soon afterwards.

Along with the case the remaining fifteen cheeses still weigh over thirty kilos. And yet I am able to lift the monster, carry it up the cellar stairs and then down the hall to the front door. I open the door and the taxi driver takes the case from me. He has the greatest difficulty in getting it four more steps into his car.

I go and put my coat on, get my hat and join the case. Mrs Peeters, our neighbour, stands at the window and follows the whole operation with the greatest interest. Upstairs I see my wife appear between the curtains.

I deposited the case in the patent store and paid off the taxi.

My cheese will is made.

I can't understand why, but my wife, who saw the taxi drawing up, didn't ask a single question and my brother seems to have no interest whatsoever in sold and unsold quantities. He talks about his patients, about my children, about politics. Has he discussed things with my wife, I wonder?

And so Hornstra will be here tomorrow.

The proceeds from the case Jan sold and from the eleven and a half rounds is ready in my office in an envelope.

Wouldn't it be best to tell my wife what awaits us tomorrow? No, she has worries enough as it is.

However much I am dreading that conversation

with Hornstra, I'm starting to long for it as a martyr yearns for redeeming death, for I imagine my prestige as a man and a father is diminishing daily. And what kind of situation is this anyway? My wife is left with a husband who is officially a clerk with General Marine, but who is playing the role of director of Gafpa, under cover of a doctor's certificate. A neurotic who has to sell cheese unheard and unseen, as though it were a crime.

And then there are the children. They show nothing of what they're feeling, but I'm sure that between themselves they are discussing that outrageous cheese fantasy as a pathological symptom. After all a father should be consistent. Whether he's a mayor, a bookmaker, a clerk or a casual labourer, is less important. But someone who does his duty for years, whatever that duty is, and then suddenly, and without being asked, starts acting out an operetta the way I did with that cheese – is he still a father?

It's definitely not normal. In this sort of predicament a minister resigns and bows out. But a husband and father can only resign by doing away with himself. And what about my brother, who has so suddenly and obviously stopped asking how sales are going? He knew from the beginning how it would turn out. So why didn't he refuse to give me that certificate? That would have been more sensible than bringing samples of medicines every day that no one needs. The wimp.

I can almost hear him asking my wife discreetly if it's over yet, the way one asks after the health of a dying man. And she probably replies that I've already taken the case out of the cellar.

I'm overcome by a frightening feeling of abandonment. What good is my family to me now? Isn't there that wall of cheese between us? If I weren't a miserable freethinker, I'd say a prayer. But can I, at the age of fifty, suddenly start praying about a cheese issue?

I suddenly think of my mother. It's lucky she has not witnessed this cheese catastrophe. Once upon a time, before she started picking kapok, she would have paid for those ten thousand cheeses to spare me this suffering.

And now I ask myself whether I deserved all this. Why did I jump on the cheese bandwagon? Was it because I was urged on by the desire to improve the lot of my wife and children? That would be noble, but I'm not that much of a saint.

Was it to cut a better figure at Van Schoonbeke's? It wasn't that either, because I'm far too vain to be satisfied by such a thing.

But why did I do it then? Cheese makes me sick. I've never wanted to sell cheese. I think it's bad enough going into a shop to buy cheese. But wandering round with a load of cheese, pleading for some Christian soul to relieve you of the burden, is something I just can't do. I'd rather be dead.

So why? It's not a nightmare – it's bitter reality. I had hoped to bury the cheeses in that patent store for ever, but they have broken out; they are looming in front of me, weighing on my soul and stinking.

I think it happened to me because I'm too easily led. When Van Schoonbeke asked me if I would take it on, I didn't have the guts to reject him and his cheese, as I should have done. And I'm paying the price of that cowardice. I deserved my cheese ordeal.

The final day has dawned.

I stayed in bed until nine-thirty and by drinking coffee slowly I got to ten-thirty. I can't read the paper. So I go to my office, the way a dog that doesn't know what to do goes to its kennel. And suddenly I have a brainwave.

Is it really necessary for me to see Hornstra in person? I can just as easily send the bit of money I owe him by post, and his cheese is safe in that store. Why not spare my wife an embarrassing scene?

At ten to eleven I sit down in our parlour next to the front door.

Perhaps he won't come at all. He may be dead. He may have gone straight on to Paris. But in that case I would have been informed, because those Dutch aren't that frivolous. He'll come later, but he will come.

Silent as a shadow, a marvellous, posh car pulls up and the bell rings.

I pull a face, because the ringing pains me, and get up.

I hear my wife put down a bucket in the kitchen and come along the hall to open the door.

As she reaches the parlour door, I leap into the hall and bar her way. She tries to get past, but I push her back. *That's* what I should have done with that cheese.

'Don't answer the door,' I hiss.

She looks at me in bewilderment, like a helpless witness to a murder. For the first time since I met her thirty years ago, she is afraid.

I don't say any more. I don't have to say anything, because she goes pale and retreats to the kitchen. I station myself in a corner of the parlour, from where I have a clear view of the street. Anyone looking in from outside can see only a dim light. Of course my neighbour is also standing in her parlour, a few feet away from me, I'm sure.

The bell rings a second time. Its imperious tones resound through my silent house.

After a wait I see the chauffeur go towards the car. He says something, opens the door, and Hornstra gets out of his car. He is wearing a check travel outfit with plus-fours and a deerstalker, and has a dog on a lead.

He looks up at my silent house front in puzzlement, comes up to our windows and tries to make out what's inside. I hear him say something, but cannot understand what.

Suddenly Mrs Peeters appears.

She's come to offer her services – of her own accord, because Hornstra did not ring her bell, otherwise I would have heard it.

She pushes her ugly face against our windows as though she can make out something where Hornstra has failed. She disgusts me. And yet she doesn't really deserve that – because what else can the poor old soul do all day long? She never goes out, and our street is her cinema, always showing the same film.

Now Mrs Peeters rings herself. And after some more gesticulation, Hornstra gets his wallet and tries to give her a tip, which she heatedly refuses. That's clear from the gesticulating.

She has not sold her soul to Hornstra, but wanted to know for her own benefit whether I'm really not home.

Well done, Mrs Peeters!

If that half-round isn't finished, I'll send Ida round to give it to her as a present.

Now Hornstra clambers back in his car, dragging his dog behind him. He slams the door and the car glides off as noiselessly as it came.

I stand there for a moment and a great feeling of acceptance fills my whole being. It's as if I'm being tucked up in bed by a loving hand.

But I have to go to the kitchen.

My wife is standing there doing nothing and looking into our back garden.

I go up to her and take her in my arms. And as my first tears fall on her weathered face, I see that she is crying too.

And suddenly the kitchen vanishes. It is night-time, and we are alone again, without children, in a secluded place, the way we were thirty years ago when we sought out a quiet spot where we could cry in peace.

The cheese tower has collapsed.

## 20

I surfaced from the deepest depths and with a sigh of relief I put the old shackle round my ankle. Today I went back to General Marine.

After such subterfuge one feels guilty, and so in order not to forfeit goodwill, I played, as well as I could, the role of someone who has actually returned to work too soon.

But it was unnecessary. I was literally inundated and Miss Van der Tak said I was wrong and should have stayed home till the end of the month. Of course she doesn't know that my wages are not being paid.

'Now you can see that there's nothing better than backgammon for someone with bad nerves,' said Tuil, giving me a cautious dig in the small of the back.

They asked me what I thought about sitting with our backs to the windows, showed me the new rolls of blotting paper, and then made me look at Hamer, because he's wearing glasses now.

Old Piet waved his hat at me from his engine like a man possessed. I slipped outside, and warmly shook his black hand, which is always covered in grease. He leaned out of his iron horse, pumped my arm so that I bounced up and down, and enthusiastically pushed his wodge of chewing tobacco from one side of his jaw to the other.

'And were the cigars good?'

He didn't even know what they had given me.

'Excellent, Piet. I'll bring a few in.'

He gave three blasts on his steam whistle in my honour and calmly continued his fifty-thousandth trip round the yard. After than I resumed my old place and got down to work.

My colleagues just give me simple order forms to type while they bang out the long specifications that are full of technical terms and quite tiring. I am given a chocolate by Miss Van der Tak every time she has one herself.

It's strange, in all those years I never realised that the office can be a congenial place. I suffocated in that cheese, while here, between two letters, I can listen to inner voices for a moment.

## 21

That same evening I wrote to Hornstra to say that for reasons of health I had been forced to give up the agency for Belgium and the Grand Duchy of Luxembourg. I added that his cheese was in one of the patent stores of the Blue Hat Haulage Company and that I was sending him the amount owing for the missing rounds by postal order. With that letter I burned my boats, since you never know when you might have another cheese urge.

Three days later I actually received an order slip from René Viaene, my agent in Bruges, stating that he had sold a total of four thousand two hundred kilos to fourteen customers. Everything had been filled in perfectly: order date, name and address of every buyer and all the other columns too.

I couldn't resist looking up his application in my letter file. It read as follows: 'I'll try to sell a bit of cheese. Yours sincerely René Viaene, Rozenhoedkaai 17,

Bruges.' There were no notes on it, since I had not called him in for an interview, as he was the only person from Bruges to offer his services. Hoping for the best, I had sent him ten order slips, just as I had to the twenty-nine others. So I shall never know if he is old or young, smart or down-at-heel, with or without a walking stick.

I passed on his order without comment to Hornstra. Perhaps I may even get my five per cent. I knew that system with the slips was good.

## 22

Van Schoonbeke phoned, because I've kept on the telephone, since I've paid for a year anyway. He asked why I've stopped coming. Hornstra has been to see him and said he was sorry he couldn't continue working with me. He had expressed satisfaction because he had found his cheese in such tiptop condition.

Did he think I would scoff the twenty tons then?

'At least we know how to store cheese in Antwerp,' said van Schoonbeke. 'And will you be coming along on Wednesday now?'

So I went back and he congratulated me.

There they all were again. The same chitchat, the same faces, but without that old lawyer with his half-round, because he's dead. In his place I saw the young Van der Zijpen, who still doesn't know if I'm prepared to go along with taking his father for those two hundred thousand little ones.

Of course van Schoonbeke has heard from my

brother that I am back in the shipyard, but he has not said anything to his friends and they go on treating me as the director of Gafpa.

The host introduces us 'Mr Van der Zijpen, Mr Laarmans.'

And we both say, 'Pleased to meet you.'

After which Van der Zijpen continues an aside with his next-door neighbour who keeps bursting out laughing.

'Don't forget to let me know as soon as you have sardines,' says the man through his teeth.

Van der Zijpen sniggers at me and asks if he should note down the order.

## 23

Today I visited my mother's grave, or rather my parents'. I go every year, but this time I brought my visit forward to help my cheese wound heal.

Buying flowers was as difficult as getting hold of a secondhand desk, because the florist had three kinds of chrysanthemums: small, medium and huge great ones, as big as loaves. And though I was eyeing the small ones, he managed to sell me the big ones, twelve of them. He wrapped them in snow-white paper and sent me packing with that huge cone that could be seen a mile off. Traipsing through town with that thing was impossible. No, really, I can't, however honourable visiting a cemetery may be. That exaggerated sheaf of flowers makes me look more ridiculous than that plaster Saint Joseph. No one buys a giant bunch of flowers like that, and it's obvious I've been taken for a ride. So into a taxi.

The cemetery is an endless affair, divided into

monotonous avenues only distinguishable by the graves and then only to an experienced eye. Main avenue, third side avenue on the left, second avenue on the right.

It must be somewhere around here. I walk, more slowly, in the direction of a black post a little further on.

Where in heaven's name has the grave got to? It's on the left, I'm sure of that. The Jacobs-De Preter Family. Miss Johanna-Maria Vandevelde. To Our Beloved Daughter Gisèle.

I break out in a sweat. Whatever must that old dear be thinking, because I can now see that the post is a praying woman. I can't ask her if she knows where my parents are buried, can I? And what am I to do if I suddenly run into one of my sisters? She'll realise that I'm hunting for our grave of course, because other-wise why would I be walking about with these flowers? Well, if that happens I'll put them on the first tombstone I find and make my getaway. Or I'll say, 'So you've come to visit too?' I'll walk along with her modestly and will get there automatically.

Ears burning, I go back to the main avenue and count again. Third on the right, second on the left. I'm back in the same avenue.

Right, I'll go on walking as if I had to get to the other side of the cemetery. I have to clasp the stalks of the chrysanthemums tightly, otherwise the flowers drag along the ground.

I tiptoe behind the woman and suddenly I see my grave. It leaps out at me, as it were. There, right next to where that old dear is praying. Kristiaan Laarmans and Adela van Elst. Thank God. It's all right if my sisters come now.

It's unbelievably peaceful here. Occasionally a droplet falls from a bare tree.

Hat off. A minute's silence.

I can relax. Those lying here have not heard a thing about my cheese story, because otherwise Mother would have come to Gafpa to cheer me up and support me.

I carefully lay my giant sheaf on the marble slab, cast a sideways glance at the black figure next to me, make a kind of bow, put my hat back on and withdraw. Five graves on, I turn into a side avenue and look back.

I stop, as if rooted to the spot. What is that creature doing at our grave? Is she going to swipe my chrysanthemums and put them on her grave? That would be a cheek.

I now see that she is removing the white wrapping, and the brownish-red splendour of the flowers appears. She spreads out my chrysanthemums and lays them on the stone slab at the front, so that the names of Mother and Father remain visible. Now she makes the sign of the cross and starts praying on *my* grave.

I duck down and creep unnoticed to the main avenue and out of the cemetery.

---

# CHEESE

I get my taxi to stop on the corner of my street, otherwise my wife will want an explanation. Because I'm not a businessman any longer. And I could easily have gone to the cemetery on the tram.

# 24

We never mention cheese again at home. Even Jan has not said a word about the case he sold so brilliantly, and Ida is like a clam. Perhaps the poor ninny is still being called 'cheese maid' at school.

As for my wife, she makes sure that no more cheese appears on the table. It was months before she served me a Petit Suisse – white, flat cheese which is no more like Edam than a butterfly is like a snake.

Good, darling children.

Dear, dear wife.

# AUTHOR'S ORIGINAL
# PREFACE

'Style is the man,' said Buffon. It's hard to imagine a more succinct and accurate way of putting it. This slogan, though, standing there like a model waiting to be immortalised by a sculptor, is not much good to a man of feeling. But is it possible to give any idea in words of what style is?

The tragic, for example, is born of a maximum of stylistic tension. Everything about the human condition itself is tragic. Think of Job's words: 'There the wicked cease from troubling, and there the weary be at rest,' and at your feet you see a mass of writhing, copulating, eating, praying humanity, with a rubbish tip next door for those whose last convulsions are over.

Style is closely allied to music, which developed from the human voice, a vehicle of rejoicing and lamentation before words on paper were thought of. Tragedy is also a matter of intensity, of tempo and harmony, of rests, alternation of exultant and slow passages and gong strokes, of simplicity and sincerity and sardonic grimaces.

Picture a sea and above it the sky. At first the blue sky is a gigantic canopy of uninterrupted splendour. Anyone taking a blue sky as their starting point must be capable of making the sky bluer than any sky has ever been in reality. The spectator must be immediately struck by the strange blue of the firmament, without being told that 'the sky is very, *very* blue'. After all, he has a soul to tell him that, style being comprehensible only to those with souls.

The sky must remain blue and pristine till the blue has fully permeated his soul. But not for *too* long, or else he'll think, 'So, the sky's blue, that's all there is to it, I've got the message.' And he'll turn his back on you and become absorbed in personal reflections. And once he's escaped your clutches you won't get him back to where he's supposed to be watching or empathising, or at least not with another blue sky. The more intense the blue the better, since then it will fill him all the sooner. And if you begin with a black sky, then the black will immediately pour all over his skin.

Once the blue splendour has lasted long enough, a first little cloud appears to remind him that he is not standing there to gaze at that blue sky for the rest of his days. And gradually the blue disintegrates into a chaos of lowering clouds.

A gong stroke heralds the first cloud and each new stroke a procession of grotesque new shapes.

The first gong stroke plays a crucial role, like the first birth in a family. The others are born in exactly the same way, but one gets used to everything, even to birth, and the element of surprise gradually diminishes.

That first gong stroke must come when everything is pure and blue, all love and happiness, when the last thing that anyone expects is a gong stroke. It should warn, unsettle, but not alarm. Something like the monastic 'Brother, you too must die' on a summer's afternoon. It must be oh so soft. The man must wonder what it was. If it was rejoicing then it was a funny way of going about it. After that first gong stroke, he must start distrusting the blue sky, like someone who suddenly tastes something odd in their food or sees something moving in the peaceful grass when there isn't a breath of wind. He must wonder if he has heard something suspicious and if that isn't perhaps a cloud there in the distance. It is best if a little later he comes to the conclusion that it wasn't a gong stroke, but that one of those rejoicing got a frog in their throat. That can only be achieved if the first stroke is soft and is not sustained for too long.

You are sitting alone at night reading in a deserted house. And you suddenly imagine you may have heard something. No, the silence persists and your heart resumes its listless rhythm.

If that first gong stroke is too loud, then nothing else that follows will have any impact. The man'll think, 'Oh, so that's the point of it? Right then.' And he will immediately block up his ears. Or he'll pit his willpower against the fairground din you are kicking up and keep his eyes wide open, knowing that soon he won't hear a thing. Because constant noise is the same as absolute silence. And the man who suddenly makes all those gong strokes himself seems like a man possessed.

After that strange blue sky has continued for a little longer, there follows a second stroke.

Next, this man of yours sees a cloud and thinks, 'So, I was right. It wasn't rejoicing.' And so as to be sure, because that blue is still on his mind, he searches his memory of what has happened for the first gong stroke. If he tries hard enough he will find it and think, 'You see, it didn't escape my attention.' However, he is still not sure if that first stroke was deliberate, it was so faint and so unexpected.

The man in his deserted house gets up and listens. And that's when they start closing in. Gradually, in an accelerating tempo, the blue is overwhelmed and massive banks of cloud pile up. The gong strokes fall thick and fast and your man can already foresee the strokes still to come. He wants to take charge himself, because he thinks he is in control and doesn't realise he is being controlled. And just when he says, 'Now comes the stroke that will bring the tower crashing down, that's what I want,' the gong falls silent and a patch of blue becomes visible.

He thinks, 'Well, it's better than I thought. It could have been worse. I could have brought the whole lot tumbling down, and that would have been the end of it.' He doesn't know that the stroke couldn't come now, because the blue has been forgotten, because the impression of the blue has been erased from his soul. And that stroke by itself is not the point, the point is the blue *and* the stroke, the blue when the stroke is expected and the stroke when one is starting to absorb the blue again.

The man in the empty house sits down again.

And when the spectator has seen the blue for the tenth time, each time more briefly, and thinks, 'Yes, now I've got it, the secret is the constant alternation of blue and masses of clouds,' *that*'s when the stroke comes. It judders right through his body and gives him goosepimples. The man in the silent house tries to get up, but can't. He is not afraid, but paralysed by the majesty of that single gong stroke. He thinks, 'You won't catch me out like that again,' and gets ready to face the next stroke, like at the circus where one always expects more pistol shots after the first one has been fired.

He's wrong, that was *the* stroke.

If you want to end with a blue sky there may be a few more strokes, but they are just a last echo, a mopping-up operation, a bird's final flutter. But if you yourself have had enough of that blue sky, then that's that, Amen and good night.

He goes on sitting there when there's nothing left, no gong strokes and no masses of cloud. Not even a blue sky.

He closes your book and leaves, forgetting his hat. On the way he stops and mutters, 'That was quite a story.' He turns back one last time, and then continues on his way in a dream and disappears over the horizon. His soul has been touched by tragic tension.

In nature, tragedy resides in the things that actually happen. In art it is more a matter of style than of what happens. A herring can be depicted tragically, even though there is nothing intrinsically tragic about such a creature. On the other hand it is not sufficient to say, 'My poor father is dead' to achieve a tragic effect.

In music the abstract nature of tragedy is seen even more clearly. The tragic quality of Schubert's 'Erlkönig' is not heightened by Goethe's words, even though a child is strangled in it. On the contrary, all that strangling distracts one from the tragic rhythm.

The same applies to literature, although there one has no scales to use but must make do with woefully inadequate words. And since every word evokes an image, the sequence of words creates a framework which can be coated with style. One cannot paint without a surface. But the framework itself is incidental, as the greatest stylistic tension can be achieved with the most insignificant of events. The whole of Rodin is just as much present in one of those hands as in the whole group of *Burghers of Calais*, and the miracle is that he was able to sustain it for seven burghers. It's just as well there weren't seventy of them. It follows that the same standard framework may be clothed so completely differently by different temperaments that no one would suspect that there was the same framework underlying such totally different products. The main thing is to have something to work with on which one can let loose one's stylistic urge in a satisfying way. That is why one should give schoolboys a choice of essay subjects and not force those fifty-seven unfortunates, all so different, to describe Spring or Mother's Funeral on the same afternoon. And if one of them were to send his teacher a letter explaining why he could not be bothered to write an essay on any subject at all, then that letter should count as his essay.

The effect one is seeking to achieve must match one's frame of mind. Someone in a genuinely happy mood should not try to evoke a tragic impression, or false notes will be struck that spoil the effect of the whole. Unless the cheerfulness is used as a foil for serious tension. But in that case there should be something odd about the cheerfulness, like the blue of that sky. Right from the opening (for a book is a song) one must keep the final chord in mind, and something of it should be interwoven through the whole story like a leitmotif through a piece of music. The reader should gradually be seized by a feeling of uneasiness, making him turn up his collar and think of his umbrella while the sun is still out in all its glory.

Those who do not lose sight of the end will automatically avoid all verbosity because they will constantly be asking themselves if each detail actually contributes to their aim. And they will soon discover that every page, every sentence, every word, every full stop, every comma either brings the object nearer or delays it. Because there is no such thing as neutrality in art. What is not necessary should be excluded and where one character will do, a crowd of them is superfluous.

In art there are no prizes for trying. Don't try to swear if you are not angry, or cry if your soul is dry, or rejoice if you aren't full of joy. One may try to bake a loaf, but one does not try to create. If there is a genuine pregnancy, birth will follow automatically, in its own good time.

*Antwerp, 1933*